P9-DGN-475

LEGEND OF THE GHOST DOG

Also by
ELIZABETH CODY KIMMEL

Secret of the Mountain Dog

The Reinvention of Moxie Roosevelt

Spin the Bottle

Lily B. on the Brink of Cool

Lily B. on the Brink of Love

Lily B. on the Brink of Paris

The Suddenly Supernatural series

Balto and the Great Race

LEGEND OF THE GHOST DOG

ELIZABETH CODY KIMMEL

SCHOLASTIC INC.

No part of this publication may be reproduced, stored in a retrieval system, or transmitted in any form or by any means, electronic, mechanical, photocopying, recording, or otherwise, without written permission of the publisher. For information regarding permission, write to Scholastic Inc., Attention: Permissions Department, 557 Broadway, New York, NY 10012.

This book was originally published in hardcover by Scholastic Press in 2012.

ISBN 978-0-545-39128-3

12 11 10 9 8 7 6 5 4 3 2   14 15 16 17 18 19/0

Printed in the U.S.A.   40
This edition first printing, September 2014

*For my expert reader Jax and
her capable assistant TR.*

DODIE

I am old now, and I have lived in this hollow near the creek all my life. When I was a girl this land was clear and open. I could watch the northern lights overhead, rippling and snaking through the night sky. Now Mother Earth is taking this place back to herself, one tree, one bush, one vine at a time. One day she will come for me too, and I will go easily enough. I am tied to this land, but they are not happy ties. When death comes for me, I will gladly go even if there is nothing beyond it, even if I will only sleep, as an old poet said, the sleep of the apples.

My childhood house is gone now, collapsed into nothing but rotting lumber, and I am sad for it — it was a good home, warm and roomy, and it was there that my family built a kennel. It was there that we raised dogs.

They were no ordinary dogs, but the best of the best. Siberian huskies. Work dogs. The same line as the great

Leonhard Seppala's famous animals. They were magnificent creatures still carrying the fierce heart of Siberia within them. They were happiest out on the trail, pulling a sled as if it were nothing more than a child's toy, racing silently over the snow as if they were gliding on top of it.

Seppala had built a kennel in Nome to breed and train his teams, and later my people did too. Puppies came every year, more than any girl could dream of having. Silla and I loved them as we loved each other, and shared them as sisters share even what does not belong to them. And our work was important, for all dogs must grow comfortable with people — they must bond with humans and mingle with them from the moment their eyes open.

Silla and I loved our job of playing with the pups. But we knew they were not pets. Though they were gentle as lambs, they were working dogs. We knew we must never, ever think of them as our own.

Not even Caspian.

We were living a dream, we just didn't know it. The rest of the world was so far from us we thought nothing could reach us on the outskirts of Nome. Certainly not the happenings in a tiny country on the other side of the world called Vietnam. But we were wrong. The war left no one untouched. Eventually all three of our brothers would be *called to serve. But Jim was the first to go, in one of the earliest waves of marines sent off to a place called Da Nang.*

A darkness had come in that year, 1965. But Silla and I pretended not to notice. Two of the dogs had litters, and Caspian was one of the pups. He was black from head to tail — a lovely, deep black that almost looked blue in the sunlight. Silla said the color reminded her of a drawing she'd seen of the darkest parts of the Caspian Sea, and that's how he got his name. We both fell in love.

Silla and I played with all the puppies, as Daddy instructed us to, but it was Caspian we went running to see each morning. Caspian knew we loved him better than the others. He was never rolling around and wrestling with the rest of them when we came down — he'd sit to one side, watching the door. He waited for us every day, always sitting there like that even if we came late.

But then that awful day came, and Caspian was never the same.

None of us were.

1

So there I was, at the very end of the earth.

Well, maybe not the *very* end. Alaska was closer to the top of the planet than I'd ever been, but it wasn't exactly the North Pole. And Nome was more isolated than any place I'd ever lived, but it was still a city.

"This place stinks!" my little brother, Jack, was yelling. "We might as well be on the moon!"

"I'd love to live on the moon," I told him. "Nice and quiet, plenty of open space, no neighbors, and a great view of the earth. Sounds perfect to me."

"Yeah," Jack retorted, jabbing a finger in my direction accusingly. "Because you are a NUT JOB!"

At the age of eight, Jack considered himself an expert in what was crazy and what was not. He made no secret of his belief that I was so far from normal I might as well have come from . . . well, the moon. And I didn't mind. There were a lot of things I'd like to be in life. But normal had never been one of them.

"Dad sent me in here to make sure you were getting unpacked," I said.

Jack grabbed a beat-up-looking suitcase near his feet, unzipped it, and hoisted it in the air. The contents spilled out all over the floor of his new bedroom in our dad's cabin.

"Done," he said.

"If you say so," I said, backing out the door.

In my own room, everything was already neatly put away. We were only supposed to be here for two weeks, but I'd brought a good selection of books, and all my warmest hiking clothes. The cabin our dad had rented was just outside of Nome. The view from my window showed an unending sea of wavy hills, with not another house in sight. I thought the place was great. Jack, on the other hand, believed we had been cruelly plopped into the center of a vast and uncivilized wilderness.

Jack and I had a week off for spring break, but we were missing an extra week of school too, since our mother was in Japan handling some corporate merger thing. The four of us couldn't go as a family to Japan and to Nome at the same time, so Jack and I had ended up with Dad, and Mom went to Japan on her own. We'd all be back together in upstate

New York soon. In the meantime, Jack liked the idea of missing an extra week of school and doing his classwork via computer. But that was the only thing he was happy about. He'd been expressing his outrage pretty much nonstop since our arrival the day before. I was supposed to be keeping an eye on him.

But I was also itching to go out and explore those hills.

"What do you say, Henry — are you up for a walk?"

My beagle was asleep at the foot of my bed. He opened his eyes at the sound of my voice and gave me a weary look, heaving a big sigh at the word *walk*. Henry's world revolved around three things: food, affection, and sleep. But once he got outside, he loved to roam as much as I did.

I made a quick trip down the hall to let my dad know I was heading out.

My father was in the tiny third room that was doubling as his bedroom and office. He was typing on his laptop when I walked in, his shaggy black and gray hair standing every which way on his head. He looked up and smiled over the top of his reading glasses when I came in. I made a mental note that he was looking a bit on the thin side — when he started writing a new book, he often forgot to eat. I'd get some kind of stew going for dinner, preferably full of sausage and vegetables. Mom had given me a longer-than-usual lecture on the phone, about how I was the one who had to take care of Dad and Jack, because they'd never do it themselves.

"How's it going, Sweet Tee?" my dad asked.

Everybody called me Tee, because I hated my full name, which is Anita. My father used variations from Sweet Tee to Hot Tee to Iced Tee, depending on my mood. Or his.

"I'm good," I said. "The prisoner in cell block J may be plotting some kind of rebellion, though."

"I consider myself warned," my father said. "I was afraid Jack wouldn't like it here. I just didn't feel like I had a choice — I can't write this book without being here to research and interview people, really live it for a while. And the firm made it pretty clear they needed your mom to be in Japan. You know. It was either Alaska, Japan, or sticking you with your grandparents."

"Believe me, you made the right choice," I said. "Jack will live. And I love it already. I was going to take Henry out for a walk, if that's okay."

"Great idea," Dad replied. "Just don't go too far. The realtor said it's easy to get turned around out there. If you get lost, you can't exactly pull over and ask for directions."

"I'll be careful," I promised. "Don't worry. And I'll be back in time to get something going for dinner."

My father smacked his head with his hand.

"I almost forgot! Joe — the guy who's going to be my research assistant — is stopping by tonight to introduce himself. I thought maybe we should ask him to stay for dinner."

"No problem," I said. "I'll make enough for four."

"Five," my father corrected. "He's going to have his daughter along with him."

"Oh," I said. "Okay, five then. Will she eat stew, do you think? Do you know how old she is?"

"No idea," he said. "I think he said she's in seventh grade, whatever that means."

My father was a real space cadet sometimes. I tried not to take it personally.

"Well, I'm in seventh grade," I reminded him patiently. "And I'm twelve. So she's probably around my age."

He looked really surprised for a moment, like I'd just solved the riddle of the Sphinx or something.

"Huh. I thought she'd be younger. Well good, you'll have somebody to hang out with then," he said.

Then he started typing again, which meant he was pretty much lost to the rest of the world for the next hour — or four.

I headed back to my room for my hiking boots and coat. I wasn't happy to hear that my dad's assistant would be bringing his daughter. Unlike Jack, I didn't want to have someone to hang out with. I was kind of picky about my friends. I was into reading and hiking the way so many girls in my grade seemed to be into clothes and celeb gossip. I had been looking forward to some quiet time in Alaska. And the last thing I wanted to do was make small talk over dinner with some bubblehead.

But I didn't have to worry about that right now. Henry perked up when he saw me lacing my boots. I layered up in a few T-shirts, then zipped myself into my thick Patagonia jacket — guaranteed to stay toasty even in Antarctica — though I was glad I wasn't going to have the chance to test that theory. Alaska in April was plenty cold enough.

"Okay, buddy, let's go!" I said to Henry, dangling his leash in the air.

Henry hopped off my bed and took his time indulging in a slow stretch, his front paws pressed into the floor and his butt extending skyward in a picture-perfect downward-facing dog. He yawned and shook himself, then sat in front of me expectantly, his huge velvety ears framing his face. Henry didn't fetch, had a weakness for digging through garbage cans, and was useless as a watchdog, but my beagle was hands down one of the most adorable-looking animals ever to grace the planet. I knelt down and hugged him, enjoying the little blast of beagle breath he sent my way as he snuffled my face, then clipped the leash to his collar.

Once we were through the front door, Henry stopped to sniff the air. There was open space in every direction, and hills and woods off in the distance. The sky seemed so vast it almost made me dizzy to look up at it. I was in completely unknown territory. Which way should I go?

Henry started pulling me to the left. I saw what his nose had already located — a worn path, leading up a series of small hills. Taking a deep breath of brisk fresh air, I followed Henry's lead.

Day one in Alaska. Off into the unknown.

2

It happened so fast I just didn't have time to react.

I had followed the old path for a good mile or so, taking my time and stopping often to get my bearings. The sky seemed so huge in Alaska, and the landscape felt far more open and remote than any I'd ever encountered hiking back at home. There was a hard edge to everything here — the sun seemed brighter, the air seemed colder, and the sky was much bluer than what I was used to. I was glad I had packed my camera. I wanted to take pictures of everything. But pictures might not fully show how it *felt* here — how vast, and wild. Wonderful, and a little dangerous.

I had reached a place where the open tundra turned to bushes and shrubs, and beyond that gave way to trees. I wasn't tired, but I had promised to take care of dinner, so I decided it was time to turn around and head back home.

Henry did not agree.

11

The path branched off into a second, much fainter trail, and Henry was very interested in something that lay in that direction. I wasn't sure what kind of wildlife lived around here, but chances were he'd gotten the scent of a rabbit or a deer.

"Come on, buddy," I told him, pulling on the leash. "You've got a nice supper waiting for you in your bowl back home, and you won't even have to run and catch it. Let's go."

Beagles are notoriously stubborn creatures, and Henry was their king. He didn't want to go back. He strained on the leash with his whole body while I pulled back in the opposite direction. It was like being in a tug-of-war with a hippopotamus. My usually devoted dog flat out refused to budge, and I made the mistake of losing my patience.

"We're going now!" I snapped, turning my back on him and taking a few steps.

Henry spun around toward me as I yanked on the leash, then suddenly began wiggling and moving backward. In one slick movement, he managed to slip out of his collar. I fell onto the grass as Henry dashed down the path.

"Henry, no!" I cried, jumping to my feet. This was bad. The few times Henry had gotten loose on hikes back home, he'd taken off for hours before returning. That's just the way beagles are. But this was not home — this was the wilderness. If Henry got lost here, he might never find his way back. He wasn't even wearing his collar and tags now. He might cross paths with a wolf, or a bear. The thought of losing my dog filled me with panic. I tore down the path after him, shouting his name.

I ran until I was so out of breath I couldn't yell for him any longer. It couldn't have been more than forty degrees out. My lungs stung with the cold and my eyes filled with tears.

"Henry!" I called hoarsely. "Come on, boy!"

The answer was silence, except for the whisper of wind moving through the trees.

The worst thing I could do was keep going forward. I wasn't going to help my dog by getting lost myself. The path ahead went over a small hill. I decided to walk to the top and have a look at the other side — one final attempt to find Henry. But after that I had no choice — I would have to turn back and go home, and trust him to use his sensitive nose to find his way back.

When I reached the top of the rise, I almost cried out with relief. Henry was at the bottom of the hill. I walked slowly and quietly toward him, not wanting him to notice me and dash off again.

13

But Henry wasn't going anywhere. He was crouched low to the ground, staring intently at something. His body was quivering. What had he found?

I walked carefully toward him, my eyes scanning the ground. When I reached him, he turned suddenly and pressed himself into my leg, whimpering. I knelt down and slipped the collar over his head. He trembled and whined softly, his eyes still firmly fixed on a spot nearby — but all I could see were a few bushes and what appeared to be an old piece of wood.

"What are you looking at, you silly boy?" I asked him, trying to keep the nervousness out of my voice. "You can't go running off like that. Come on, let's get home. I'll get your supper."

Henry had lost all of his bullish strength. He meekly followed me back up the hill, his head down and his tail firmly between his legs. As we reached the top I turned to glance back one more time. This time I noticed something — movement in the brush, a glimpse of something sleek and dark as a shadow. Though I couldn't make out what it was, I had the distinct feeling I was being watched. A little shudder ran up my spine, and in one fluid movement the thing was gone, like a sea serpent returning to the depths.

My heart pounding, I retraced my steps back to the main path without any trouble. Henry perked up a little as we made our way back home, but I was still troubled by what I'd seen.

Or what had seen me.

What in the world was back there, staring at me so hard I could feel it? My stomach rumbled, and I realized I was starving, on top of being scared silly.

I'd have to leave the mystery to be investigated some other day.

3

There was an old Jeep parked in our driveway behind Dad's car.

"Oh, great," I grumbled to Henry. "Looks like our company is here already."

But Henry loved company. He'd mostly recovered from his earlier scare and was trotting happily toward the driveway. He paused by the Jeep, gave the wheel a few sniffs, then lifted a leg to leave what my dad calls one of his "free samples" on the tire.

"Henry, how rude! Were you raised in a barn?" I asked him sternly.

Henry gazed up at me, his liquid brown eyes wide. A piece of grass was stuck to the end of his nose. He was the picture of adorable innocence, like he'd just tumbled out of a Disney movie. I bent down and planted a kiss on his soft head.

16

"Well, buddy, at least *you'll* enjoy the party," I said. "Let's go in and face the people."

I heard the sound of voices as soon as I walked in the front door. There was also the smell of something cooking. I unclipped the leash and Henry dashed to the back of the house, where the kitchen, dining room, and living room all shared a single open space around a wood-burning stove. I followed Henry into the room.

"And here's Tee now," I heard my father say.

Dad was sitting on the couch with a big, cheerful-looking man I presumed was Joe the Research Assistant. Jack was standing at one end of the couch, his hands on his hips. He was staring at Joe like the guy was an alien who had just beamed onto the furniture — one that hadn't yet declared himself a friend or a foe.

"Hi, Tee," the man said, standing and extending a hand. "I'm Joe. Very glad to meet you."

"Nice to meet you too," I said, shaking his hand. Joe looked about ten years younger than my father, with a shock of red-gold hair and a round, ruddy face. His bright blue eyes were open and friendly. He smiled and nodded, then sat back down without asking me any of the usual Irritating and Predictable Adult Questions — how old are you? what are you studying? how do you like school? Henry approached

17

Joe and began to energetically lick one of his pant legs, leaving a slimy smear on the fabric. Joe grinned and reached down to scratch my dog between the ears.

I decided Joe was okay.

"He brought chili," Jack declared. "And brownies!"

I glanced over at the kitchen, which was really just a corner of the living room that had a stove and a sink. Sure enough, there was a huge yellow pot simmering on the stovetop. It smelled great.

"So you're off duty tonight, Tee," my dad said. "Tee's usually our chef when their mom is away on business — without her, Jack and I would be eating nothing but Pop-Tarts all day."

"Which would be *awesome*!" Jack declared.

"Chili's great," I told Joe. "I'll heat up bread and grate some cheese."

"Thanks, Sweet Tee," my father said. "Joe, if you want to come look now, I can show you some of the material I've already put together, and a list of what I'm still looking for."

Jack got up to go with them.

"How come they call it *re*-search? Is that like a do-over?" I heard my little brother asking Joe as I walked to the fridge. "Can you find out if there are flying saucers here?

Can you figure out secrets when people don't want you to? If I want to call the president, can you get his phone number?"

Joe paused in the doorway and looked at me.

"Thanks for the assist, Tee," he said. "I'll just leave you and Quin to get acquainted at your own speed."

It was only then that I noticed the girl sitting on the floor in the corner of the room, her nose buried in a book. She had the same red-gold hair as Joe, except hers hung in a long, fat braid over one shoulder. She glanced up at the sound of her name, making brief eye contact with me. As her father left the room, she returned her attention to her book without saying a word. Henry trotted over to her, sat down, and stared at her. Quin calmly turned a page and continued reading.

Okay then.

I didn't need to make small talk, either. I got a brick of cheese out of the fridge and began grating it into a bowl. When I had more than even Jack could consume in one sitting, I pulled a loaf of bread from the bread box and stuck it in the oven to warm. I poked around in the cupboard, eventually finding five bowls of varying sizes and designs, and I placed them on the table.

Quin still hadn't moved. Henry was sitting next to her, watching her quietly. Usually my dog couldn't resist hurling himself on new people, attempting to climb them to examine every available inch with his wet, pink tongue. I had never seen him sit so respectfully next to a stranger. I felt an irritating twinge of jealousy.

I picked up his bowl.

"Henry. Ready for some hoosh?" I asked, using the word for meat stew that the old polar explorers had used. We learned about that when my father wrote a book on the South Pole, and after that *hoosh* became the default world for all of Henry's meals.

Henry's ears pricked up and he gave me an interested look. But he didn't come scampering over as he usually did at the mention of food. Quin turned another page and Henry returned his gaze to her. Shifting the book into one hand, Quin reached over and stroked the beagle's back, her eyes still on the page. Henry's tail wagged wildly at the attention. My twinge of jealousy upgraded itself to a full-blown pang.

I poured Henry's kibble loudly into his bowl, then shook it for added emphasis.

"Henry! Hoosh!"

The magic combination of sight, sound, and the scent of doggy kibble finally spurred my dog to his feet. He trotted over to me, but when I put his bowl on the floor, he didn't attack it in his customary feeding frenzy.

It was almost unheard of for Henry to lose his appetite. I forgot about Quin and her magical effect on my dog, and knelt down to feel Henry's nose.

"What's wrong, buddy? Don't you want to eat? Are you still upset about before?"

"What happened before?"

Ah. She speaks.

"I don't know — nothing really," I told Quin. "I took him for a hike to do some exploring. He slipped his leash after about a mile and took off down another trail. When I found him, he was acting weird."

Quin put her book down.

"Weird how?" she asked.

I hardly knew the answer myself, and it seemed strange to suddenly be having a conversation with the formerly silent Quin. But I was intrigued by the effect she had on Henry. Plus, she lived around here. Maybe she'd know what spooked him so thoroughly.

"He was crouched really low to the ground, and he was shaking and whimpering. He seemed to be staring at something, but I couldn't see anything at all. Just a couple of bushes and part of an old fence."

Quin watched Henry thoughtfully. He was still ignoring the food, though a few telltale beads of drool had gathered in the corner of his mouth.

Quin put her book down and got to her feet. Henry looked up at her and thumped his tail a few times as she walked over. She knelt next to him, running her hands slowly down his back, her eyes half-closed. I knelt down too. He was my dog, after all.

"He's still shaking a little," she said. "What trail were you on?"

"I don't know," I said. "We picked it up right by the house and it headed, well, mostly west, I guess."

"Sounds like you might have been near Dorothy Creek," Quin said. "Some miners built cabins there back during the gold rush — they thought there was gold in the creek bed. There are more abandoned mines and cabins around here than anyone really knows. There are stories . . . there are things out there that would spook any dog."

"Things?" I asked. "Like animals? I thought maybe it was a snake or something."

"I'm not talking about other animals," Quin said.

"Well, then . . . what?"

She didn't answer.

The sound of my father and Joe laughing boomed from the other room. Henry seemed to be listening to Quin, his head cocked to one side and his eyes on her face.

"It isn't FUNNY!" I heard Jack yell. I knew all of Jack's voices, and I could tell he was genuinely upset about something. Moments later, a door slammed hard. Henry made a tiny, puppylike noise in his throat. Quin's hands were still on his back. She squeezed his haunches gently, and he gazed up at her.

It was everything I could do to stop myself from snapping, *Get off my dog!* I couldn't help it. When it came to Henry, I was definitely the jealous type.

My father appeared in the doorway.

"Tee, Jack's gotten himself in a state about something. Can you go talk to him? He's in his room."

I stood up with a quiet sigh.

"Sure," I said.

Quin murmured something to Henry, rubbing one palm in a circle over the base of his spine. He got to his feet, took a step toward his bowl, and began eating his food.

What was this girl, some kind of beagle whisperer?

At least Henry was eating now. That should be the only thing that mattered.

Quin was strange, and aloof, and maybe even rude. But Henry liked her. He was finally eating his dinner. I wanted to dislike Quin, but something wouldn't let me.

I had to figure out how to get her to tell me exactly what she meant. About the kind of thing that could scare my dog, but wasn't a person — wasn't any kind of animal at all.

DODIE

When the latch on the puppies' kennel was not fastened properly, the gate could swing open in the wind. It might have been Silla who was responsible, or it might have been me. To this day I don't know. I just know we were wakened before dawn by the sound of every dog, pup and adult, barking at the top of their lungs. They only did that when something was circling the kennel, and only two creatures ever stalked the dogs' enclosure. Bears and wolves.

We all ran down together, my folks, Silla and I, and our brother Jim, who was temporarily home on leave from Vietnam. The sky was dark, and I remember seeing the northern lights in the sky — the amazing living ribbon of color and energy that usually left me breathless. But today, I was breathless from fear. Whatever had frightened the dogs had run off, but the gate to the pups' pen was wide open.

For one terrible moment I thought they were gone, every last one of them. But when Daddy shone the light inside I saw them huddled in a corner of the pen, one on top of the other. Only one of them was missing.

Caspian.

Daddy locked up the pens tight, and Silla and Jim and I went calling for Caspian as loud as we could. We were desperate, Silla and I — both of us knew something had happened to him. It was as if his fear had been written in the wind — we could feel it, fresh, like the smell of blood. Silla begged Daddy to let us go into the woods to look, because she felt Caspian was lying there, hurt — that he couldn't get back to us on his own. But Daddy wasn't going to let his fragile young daughters venture into the woods, even with Jim as protection. He did not even permit us to take walks there near the creek, where the treeline began.

When I was a child I thought there wasn't a thing in the world my father was afraid of, but I came to learn he was afraid of those woods. Silla kept pleading with him to let her go after Caspian, and he kept refusing, and as we were still all standing around arguing I saw Caspian creeping toward us, dragging himself, really, from the border of the woods toward the kennel path.

We could all see something had been after Caspian, and had taken a pretty good bite of him. He was limping and exhausted and his neck was bloody. But there was something more than that — it was the way he was creeping, low to the ground. Whatever had happened to Caspian out there, whatever had gone after him, it was plain to me and Silla that the dog was terrified. I felt it too — the same terror that was in Caspian's eyes vibrated deep within my core. He was only a pup, still just four or five months old. Anybody who worked with dogs would know immediately to stand still, to be calm, to not rush Caspian or frighten him. Anybody would know that.

But Jim had been away many long months, being a soldier instead of a dog handler, and it seemed to me he'd come home on leave almost as frightened as Caspian. Maybe he just forgot what he knew about dogs, or maybe it was something else, maybe the war had just changed him and he couldn't read the dogs anymore.

Whatever it was, when Jim saw Caspian, he lunged at him. Maybe he just meant to grab Caspian's collar so the pup couldn't run off again. But he scared Caspian.

What happened next was over in a flash. Caspian snarled and leapt at Jim and sank his teeth into his arm. Silla and I screamed at Caspian to let go, and my father hollered and swung a stick, landing a stinging blow on Caspian's back. Caspian did let go of Jim then, and for one terrible second or two I thought he might attack my father. It was the only moment in my life I ever doubted Caspian, and I will regret it until the day I die.

4

I sat on the edge of the couch studying the map, growing hot in the layers of fleece and long underwear I had put on. The Dorothy Creek trail was not too far from our cabin — in fact I was pretty sure Henry and I had been on it for a while, before Henry had taken off. According to the trail map there was a waterfall at the end of it, but it was probably too far to go today. From where our cabin was located, I probably wouldn't even make it to the mouth of the creek, but I was going to try.

It was noon and the thermometer read just thirty-one degrees Fahrenheit. Fortunately the sky was cloudless and the sun blazing. I figured that as soon as Henry and I got going briskly enough, I'd be taking off some of my fleece layers.

"Henry! Walkies!" I called.

Henry, who had been lying as still as a rock near the wood-burning stove, looking as if he'd been deep in a coma for some time, sprang to his feet.

I laughed. It must be amazing to live like a dog, totally in the moment. Whatever was going on at that very second, it was all about that and nothing else for Henry. So completely uncomplicated.

"Okay, buddy, let's get your leash," I said.

Henry shot in a quick circle on hearing the word *leash*, then stopped, staring at me intently and wagging his tail so hard I was surprised he didn't propel himself forward all the way out of the room.

"Wait, I'm coming too!" Jack called.

Tell me I did not just hear that, I thought.

A walk alone with Henry meant time to think, and the freedom to stop whenever I felt like it if something caught my eye — the ripple of wind through leaves, or the unique formation of a tree trunk. I loved to take photographs when I hiked at home, and I was even more eager to get some great shots of the Alaskan wilderness, which was like nothing I'd ever seen before. Jack had no patience for the time I took setting up a shot — he would chatter and complain and spoil my concentration.

Even if I wasn't taking photographs, a walk with Jack meant endless requests for food, and complaints about the speed and direction of the walk, along with more general gripes about the temperature, the itchiness of hats, the ridiculous and unfair reason he was the only human on the planet not to have the newest PlayStation.

"You don't really want to come with me," I told my little brother, who had run into the room holding three fleeces, two of which were Dad's. "You'll be tired in ten minutes and wanting to turn back, just like always."

"No, I wanna go!" he protested. "I won't get tired, I promise! I read online that there's all kinds of cool stuff in Alaska — wolves and bears and snakes. And Joe said Alaska's so big sometimes you can still find a new animal nobody ever even heard of before! If I did that, they'd have to name it after me, right? Right, Tee?"

I sighed. I knew my brother well enough to know he was set on coming with me. And though Dad was home and working in his office today, there was no real reason I couldn't be the awesome big sis I was and let Jack tag along. He'd get tired and quit and I could have another hike later by myself, if I felt like it.

"Okay. But you have to listen to the rules first," I said.

"Rules?" Jack asked. "You don't get to make rules."

"I didn't make them, Jackster. They're from the packet of trail maps I got. We're not in Woodstock anymore. There are special rules for hiking in Alaska, and if you're going to come with me, you have to listen to what they are first."

Jack looked dubious, but he sat on the couch expectantly.

Henry raced back into the room, saw the two of us sitting, and flung himself to the floor in heavy exasperation. I opened the envelope of trail maps and pulled out the Hikers' Guide.

"One: Always travel with an up-to-date trail map and a compass or GPS device. Two: Always have more water than you think you'll need, and a well-packed first-aid kit. Protein bars are also recommended. Three: Dress warmly in layers, with appropriate hiking boots and socks. Check the weather service for updates immediately before leaving."

"This is boring," Jack complained. "And I can't carry stuff — I'm too small."

"Shush," I said. "I'll bring the pack. You have to listen to all the rules or you can't come. There are only two more."

Jack sighed and made a face. Henry was looking at me so intently he seemed about to levitate off the floor.

"Four: Tell someone what trail you will be hiking, and when you expect to return. Five: If you encounter any wildlife, keep a safe distance and be respectful. Bear sightings are rare in this area, but move away quickly if you see one, making as much noise as possible."

"Cool!" Jack yelled. "We might see a bear? That would be epic! What if it chases us? It would eat you first, 'cause you're bigger, right? This is going to be so rad!"

I tried to hide my smile.

"Just put your layers on," I said. "That blue fleece is Dad's, you know. Find yours."

Jack raced out of the room.

"And a hat and gloves, with the mitten shells!" I called after him.

Henry was standing directly in front of me, literally quivering with anticipation.

"I'm sorry," I said, kneeling down and giving him a hug. "I told you we were going, then we didn't go. Come on — let's get your leash."

Ever in the moment, Henry had forgotten that I'd disappointed him in the very recent past. He jumped up and executed a perfect pirouette of excitement, then dashed down the hall to the place by the front door where I kept his leash.

I grabbed a second bottle of water from the fridge and followed Henry to the front door, stowing the bottle in my pack.

"Let's go!" Jack said, his voice coming from behind me.

I stood up and looked him over. He'd found his own fleeces, but at least one of them was on backward. In one hand he held his coat, and I could see his gloves and mittens were all crammed in one small pocket. At least he'd put on a hat — Jack had a legendary hatred of hats, and this one had been especially purchased for him to wear in Alaska. It was a purple and white Scandinavian-style winter hat with two colorful tassels hanging down the front. The price tag had not yet been removed. I had to give credit where credit was due — the kid was trying.

"You look great," I said, helping him zip up his coat and sort out his gloves and the fat mittens that went on over them. A small, mischievous part of me decided to leave the price tag on the hat.

"Come on!" Jack said. "We're gonna miss everything!"

I loved that Jack thought there was some kind of schedule of wildlife in the Alaskan wilderness.

"You're forgetting one of the rules," I said, putting my hands on my hips.

Jack's forehead momentarily creased, then his face brightened.

"Dad, we're going!" he yelled.

I walked past my brother and opened the door to Dad's office.

"We're going to head up the Dorothy Creek trail for a mile or two," I told him. "I don't think we'll get that far, and we can take the loop that heads back toward home if Jack gets tired."

Our father was sitting at a small desk overflowing with papers. His laptop had been put on a chair off to one side. He was an old-school writer — he needed to have stuff on paper, in spite of the monumental disorganization that came with it. He took off his glasses and squinted at me, rubbing his eyes.

"That's great. That's really great that you're taking Jack along — you're aces, kid."

"Thanks," I said, warming at the praise. "I'll figure out dinner when we get back."

In the hallway, Jack was practically jumping up and down. He had Henry's leash clipped to his collar. Henry looked at me with pleading eyes, his expression saying, *Now? We're going now, right?*

"Let's go!" I said, throwing open the heavy front door.

The sunlight was absolutely brilliant. The small, undulating hills stretched in every direction. There were no trees nearby, but I knew they were out there — at least in the direction I'd gone the first day. We would start on the same trail that led north from the cabin, and the Dorothy Creek route was a wide, gravely trail we'd hit soon.

"How come we're going this way?" Jack asked.

"'Cause this is the way we're going," I told him. That was the kind of logic Jack understood, and he accepted it without pestering me further.

I took a deep breath, filling my lungs with the crisp, fresh air. It was hard to get used to how cold it was here — it was April, after all. But the sun was powerful and warmed my face, its brightness giving the illusion there was more warmth in the air. After a few minutes of energetic walking, my body was heating up anyway.

"You're going too fast," Jack complained. "How come we have to go uphill all the time?"

"Well, because the trail is going uphill," I said. "It leads up to that little ridge up there."

Henry wasn't having any problem with the hill — he was straining on his leash so hard it was like being on one of those rope tows that pull you up a ski slope.

"Here, take Henry," I said, offering Jack the leash, which he carefully took, putting his hand through the loop and wrapping it around his wrist as I'd taught him.

"Wow!" Jack exclaimed, as Henry surged upward. "I don't have to do anything!"

"Yep, just don't let go of him, and don't fall down," I said.

Now I could walk in peace, as Jack happily experimented with how far he could lean back and still be pulled up the hill by our beagle. My legs felt strong, and the sun was delicious on my face. When we reached the ridge, there really wasn't all that much to see, just more hills, and in the faraway distance, the snow-capped Kigluaik Mountains. We walked in silence for a long time. I would have happily gone on like that for several hours. But when the sun went behind a cloud and the air suddenly felt cold, Jack stopped.

"I'm tired," he said. "I want to go home."

It usually made me nuts when Jack did this — bugged me to let him tag along someplace with promises that he wouldn't get bored or tired, only to become exactly that.

But I was in a great mood. We still had almost two weeks left in Alaska, tons of time to explore, to read, to have all the quiet time I needed.

"Tee, I'm tired," Jack repeated.

"Okay," I said. "We should be coming up on a turnoff soon — that will be the old miner's trail — and it loops right back to the cabin. We'll be home in a half hour, maybe less."

"A half hour?" Jack grumbled, but it wasn't real grumbling, I could tell. He knew I could have forced him to keep hiking if I'd wanted to.

"Downhill is much easier than uphill," I reminded him.

We found the turnoff more or less where I thought we would, and looped back south. The path was wide here, with gravel and stone and weeds growing through it. It was easy going and we were making good time when Henry came to an abrupt stop and Jack almost fell right over him.

"Hey, stupidy-dumb dog!" Jack exclaimed. *Stupidy-dumb* was Jack's current catchall insult.

"He's smarter than you are," I said, but I was watching Henry curiously.

"He is not," Jack retorted.

Henry was standing statue still, his tail extended and his nose in the air. He seemed to be listening for something with every cell in his body. Or maybe listening wasn't quite the right word. Expecting. Everything about my dog said he was on full alert.

I looked around. I couldn't be sure, but it seemed like we might be close to the spot where Henry had been spooked the day before. I could see a good distance up the trail from where we were standing, to where a copse of willow bushes began and gave way to trees.

Then I saw it, a shadow moving along the bushes, low to the ground but definitely not small in size. The hackles on Henry's back stood up, and he tried to growl but it turned quickly to a whimper. The shadow stopped, as if it had heard Henry. For a moment it seemed as if the world stood still, my beagle frozen in place, the dark shape by the willow bushes unmoving. A chill ran up my spine.

"What? What's Henry doing?" Jack asked.

It was as if the sound of his voice broke the spell. The shadow shape melted into the willow bushes. Henry's stance relaxed slightly.

"It's nothing," I said. "He's just hungry. Come on, let's get home."

I took the leash from Jack and walked quickly in the direction of home. I only looked back once, as we were about to go down the next rise.

I could see nothing but the unremarkable line of willow bushes.

And yet I knew something was there, watching me.

5

I'd meant to go back out later that afternoon without Jack, but something stopped me. Maybe it was the animal — or shadow — or whatever we'd seen. The feeling that something might have been stalking me, hunting me. Or maybe the hike was just more tiring than I thought. Instead I played solitaire, cooked a decent dinner, and then the three of us watched a movie late into the night.

I awoke at my usual hour the next morning, but I had a feeling Jack was down for the count. We'd gotten a lot of exercise on our hike, and then he'd stayed up late. Even normally, he didn't like to get up before eleven.

"So Joe is coming by to pick me up, and we're heading over to the local historical society," my father told me over bowls of cereal. "The guy there says they have boxes and boxes of letters and news clippings about mushers and their dogs, but none of it is catalogued. We're just going to have to look through it piece by piece, see if there's anything we can use."

He sighed, frowned, and rubbed his forehead with his hand. My father wanted his book to focus on the evolving relationship between human and dog in Alaska, how they had depended on each other, and how that way of life was disappearing because of the snowmobile. But he was stuck — he kept saying he needed something or someone to appear with a completely fresh perspective, to breathe life into his book. Problem was he had no idea who or what that was.

The cabin smelt of freshly brewed coffee, and I'd mixed up some frozen orange juice in a pitcher.

"Okay," I said, pulling the carton of half-and-half from the refrigerator and adding enough to my coffee to turn it a light beige. I loved that my dad let me drink coffee. When he sat sipping his each morning he looked so pensive, like the writer he was. Having my own cup made me feel almost the same way. "When do you think you'll be back?"

"Hard to say," he said, getting up and walking over to the kitchen cupboards. "Don't keep dinner waiting, though."

I blinked once, processing what he'd just said, and put my mug on the counter quietly.

"Dinner?" I asked him. "You're going to be gone the whole day?"

He turned and looked at me, confused.

"Well, yeah," he said. "Unless . . . is there something else I should be doing?"

He looked like the classic absentminded professor — his mane of gray-black hair uncombed, his face stubbly and in need of a shave, his eyes magnified somewhat by the thick lenses of his glasses. He looked so lost in the real world sometimes, which made me feel protective of him.

"No, of course not," I said quickly. "I mean, that's what you're here to do, and everything. I just wanted to make sure I had it straight. I'll come up with some kind of plan for Jack, and make sure he goes on the school website to get his classwork."

I added a smile, so my father could see that I wasn't trying to be whiny.

In truth, I'd hoped to get back out on the trail today, maybe pack a blanket and a few books and find a nice quiet spot to read and take some photographs. When Jack was around, the concept of quiet simply didn't exist. But there was still plenty of time — it would keep for another day.

"That's great," my father said, giving me an affectionate smile before turning to rummage through the cabinet again. "And you know, you don't have to be Jack's constant companion the whole time we're here. Take some time for yourself, kiddo."

I grinned.

"I will," I said. "I'm going to hang that hammock we brought. That will be my personal reading spot, and I'm going to make a sign that —"

The end of my sentence was drowned out by the chink of ceramic striking ceramic as Dad started rooting through the cabinet again.

"What are you looking for?" I asked him, perplexed.

"The old Barnes & Noble mug I packed," he said. "The huge one. For my coffee."

"Dad," I said, pointing at the kitchen table.

He turned to look at me, then his gaze shifted to where I was pointing. The mug he was looking for was sitting there in plain view, filled with steaming coffee. I was pretty sure he'd already taken a few sips out of it.

He gave me his most sheepish look.

"Oh," he said. "And my head?"

"On your shoulders," I assured him.

"And it's Saturday today, right?"

"Tuesday," I corrected.

"That one I knew," he shot back. "I was just testing you."

I laughed.

"If you say so," I told him.

He headed back toward the table, stopping to give me a hug first. I loved the way he smelled — of sage shampoo and Ivory soap and Halls menthol cough drops, which he consumed in enormous amounts starting with the moment he got up in the morning.

"Don't know what I'd do without you, daughter of mine," he said. "Hey, do we have half-and-half?"

"Already in your coffee," I said.

I heard what sounded like gravel crunching under tires, and moments later Henry began to bark.

"Oh boy, that's probably Joe," my dad said. "I really like him, but I think he's obsessed with schedules. Making them . . . and keeping them. He's got this thing about being on time. It may be his fatal flaw."

"I'll put the coffee in a thermos if you want to go get your stuff," I offered.

"Yep, perfect," he said. "Then we'll get out of here. Oh," he called over his shoulder from the hallway, "Joe said to tell you not to worry about lunch. Quin's bringing her own since she's a vegetarian."

Quin would be here? For the whole day? More details that had slipped through the cracks. I sighed as I got my father's thermos out of the cabinet to give it a quick rinse.

Whatever. If the girl wanted to sit in the corner with her face in a book for the next eight hours, it was no skin off my nose.

I heard a knock, and the sound of the front door squeaking open, followed by the clatter of a dog scrambling into the hallway.

"Henry!" I heard Joe exclaim. "How you doing, you handsome hound?"

I walked into the hallway to greet them. Joe was crouched down, rubbing Henry's back and cheerfully submitting to having his face licked. I had warmed to Joe on sight, and this only reinforced my feeling that he was a good guy.

Quin, on the other hand, gave me no such warm and fuzzy feeling. She stood behind her father, shifting her weight from one foot to the other and looking uncomfortable. When our eyes met, she didn't smile or indicate that she knew me in any way. I might as well have been a mailbox.

"Are you sure you guys are going to be okay here on your own?" Joe asked, looking from me to Quin as he rubbed Henry's head. Henry made a little oink of pleasure.

"We're fine," Quin said. "I brought two books."

She walked past me toward the living room, leaving me standing there, somewhat awkwardly, with her father.

"Sorry," Joe said. "She doesn't mean to be rude. She's just kind of . . . out of practice with people. She's been homeschooled for the past couple of years, so she's not usually around kids her own age."

"That's okay," I said. I wasn't wild about Quin, but I definitely liked her father, and I wanted him to like me. "I'm kind of a loner myself. One of my favorite quotes is 'I do not want people to be very agreeable, as it saves me the trouble of liking them a great deal.'"

Joe looked delighted.

"Jane Austen!" he said. "Quin is nuts over her. You know, you two might actually get along!"

Don't hold your breath, I thought. But I smiled at Joe.

"I'm sure we will," I said.

My father came out of his study stuffing papers into an old leather satchel, his battered laptop tucked under one arm.

"Okay, I think I'm ready," he said.

"Let me grab your thermos," I said, dashing back toward the kitchen. As I grabbed it, I noticed Quin had curled up on the couch and already seemed lost in a book. I headed back to the hallway.

"Here you go," I said, holding it out.

My dad almost dropped the laptop reaching for the coffee.

"I'll take it," Joe said. "I'm beginning to think it's a good thing I'm driving."

"Me too," I said with a grin. "Dad is an unbelievably bad driver. Not just cars, either. Bikes, mopeds — even those bumper cars they have at carnivals. If it's got a steering wheel, he'll crash it into something."

"I'd take that very personally if it didn't happen to be true," my father said. "Okay, I think we're good to go. I've got the satellite phone, Tee — emergencies only, though. I don't want to broker any disputes today."

"Gotchya," I said, holding the door open and watching as the two of them headed down the path to the driveway, already lost in conversation.

Birds of a feather, I thought. *Dad's going to have a blast.*

I shut the door. Jack was still in his room, and I decided to let sleeping little brothers lie for the time being. But it seemed weird to just pretend Quin wasn't in the house, so I went back to the living room. This time she looked up from her book when I walked in.

"You don't need to try to bond with me or anything," she said. "I've got plenty of reading material. I'm not very entertaining, but I'm low maintenance."

I laughed a little, but it came out sounding weird.

"Okay," I said. I started to wipe down the kitchen counters and rinse out the coffee press. The cabin seemed uncomfortably silent, and the sound of Quin turning a page was bizarrely amplified. It felt harder to not talk.

"So I hear you like Jane Austen," I said, tossing the sponge into the sink.

"Yep," Quin said.

"Me too," I told her. "I love everything she's done."

Quin peered at me over the top of her book.

"What, like the movies?" she asked.

"No!" I exclaimed, genuinely offended. "The books."

Quin gave a small nod.

"Which is your favorite?" she asked.

"*Persuasion*, definitely," I told her.

"Hard to argue with that," Quin said. "Do you like Wilkie Collins?"

"Are you serious? I love him. I've read *The Moonstone* like three times."

"Huh," Quin said. "That's pretty cool."

I got the feeling I'd passed some kind of preliminary test. I had no idea why I suddenly cared what Quin thought of me. But I did. Maybe it was simply because I'd found a fellow bookworm.

48

I knew girls my age who were really into reading. But not the kind of stuff I was into — Empire dramas and Victorian gothic mysteries. I loved books as much as I loved dogs. I was starting to think Quin might feel the same way. This was a first for me. I sat down on the other end of the couch.

"Do you live in Nome?" I asked.

"For now," she said. "My dad teaches some classes at Northwest community college. This is his third semester, but you never know when they're going to decide they don't want the classes anymore. Then we go where the work is. But we've been here since I was ten."

I nodded.

"How is it living here?"

Quin shrugged.

"Okay, I guess. Not too many people, which is good. I like being alone. Most of the time, anyway. Every once in a while I get a case of the creeps."

I remembered what Quin had said the other day. About "things."

"What do you mean?"

Quin hesitated a moment, then shrugged. She turned her eyes back to the book on her lap.

"I'm not crazy," she said.

"I didn't say you were," I told her. How did we get to crazy?

Quin turned a page and I felt a flash of irritation. She was the one who'd brought the subject up, not me.

"I've just been wondering, you know," I said. "About what happened with my dog the other day? Something just felt really off about the whole thing. Like something's not right in that part of the woods."

"He probably just saw a snake or something," Quin said, flipping another page.

"No, I don't think so," I countered. "I went out again with him yesterday. My little brother came too, so it wasn't much of a hike. But something happened again. Henry wasn't exactly spooked that time. But the thing is, I kind of was."

Quin's eyes stayed on her book, but I could tell she was listening to me.

"Henry alerted, you know, the way a dog would if he suddenly smelled a rabbit or a deer or something?"

Quin's eyes were on mine now, her gaze direct and interested. She nodded.

"And I'm not sure, but I don't think we were very far from the place he got scared the first time. But like I said, Jack was along, and I didn't want to scare him. So we headed home, and I didn't say anything. But I'm pretty sure I saw something out there."

"Something?" Quin asked. "What was it?"

"I don't know. It looked like a shadow. But it moved like an animal. And it was almost like it knew Henry was there. As if they were . . . checking each other out, almost. And then it disappeared, just kind of melted into the brush. But even after that, I felt like it was still there. Like it was watching me."

Quin put her book down and gave me a long look. I had probably said too much. I probably sounded crazy.

"And I'm not crazy, either," I said defensively.

"That's obvious," Quin replied.

That disarmed me. I sat down next to her on the couch.

"What did you mean the other day when you said there were things out there that would scare any dog?" I asked.

Quin hesitated just a moment, like she needed to be sure about me. Then she pushed the book away and rearranged herself, sitting crossed-legged like a Buddha.

"Alaska is full of stories, history, weird stuff. Like any other place, I guess. A lot of people came out to this area during the gold rush, and nobody really knows for sure what happened to all of them. There are plenty of ghost stories, and people say there's a witch living way out in the woods, the usual stuff. But I was thinking of something specifically, actually, a legend I've heard a friend of my dad's tell about Dorothy Creek."

"What about it?" I asked.

"It's not even a story, really," Quin said. "He just said that people have seen something out where the trees grow thickest. The legend goes you're mostly likely to see it when the northern lights are in the sky, but I've heard of people seeing stuff in the middle of the day too. Some kind of phantom or wraith, they usually say. Watching them. Nobody seems to agree just what it is — wild animal, wolf, something like that. I just know that over the years people have seen it, longer than any one animal should be able to stay alive, and I've heard it described just like that — dark, and you never quite get a glimpse of it. People call it Shadow."

Quin twisted her braid around one hand, watching me with clear blue eyes.

I felt the familiar chill creep up my spine. I had told Quin I wasn't crazy, but secretly I had to kind of wonder. Anyone would.

But now I knew other people had seen it too. Other people had felt watched. Whatever it was, the Shadow was real.

"Weird that you encountered it two days in a row, though," Quin added. "You had Henry with you both times?"

I nodded.

"The Shadow thing could be drawn to the dog. Dogs have a really distinctive energy. Other animals can sense it."

"You think this . . . Shadow . . . is haunting my dog?" I asked.

"I don't know. Maybe. It's not something I can figure out by thinking about it. I'd have to see it."

"Oh," I said, disappointed.

"Take me there," Quin suggested.

"Really? Right now?" I asked.

She nodded.

"But . . . I can't just go off right now. Jack is still asleep. I practically had to swear out an affidavit to my mom before we left, saying I'd keep an eye on him. And, believe me, you wouldn't want him tagging along. And he's got homework."

"But you just said he's asleep now," Quin pointed out.

"Well, yeah," I said. "He pretty much never wakes up if I don't dump something on him."

Quin glanced at her watch.

"It's only nine thirty," she said. "We can be there and back before he wakes up. Your mom can't expect you to keep an eye on him while he's sleeping, can she? Get Henry and take me to the spot, and let's see if it happens again."

"I just . . . I mean, Jack's a really sound sleeper, but still — I don't know."

"Did anyone specifically say not to leave him alone at all, even if he was sleeping?" Quin pressed.

I hesitated.

"No," I said.

"So geez, what's the problem? It's not like we're in some big city here — there's no one around for miles. He'll be fine. And if you already have to spend half your day watching him, shouldn't you grab the chance to get out while you have it?"

Everything Quin said was true, but I still had an uncomfortable feeling in my stomach. And yet . . . I really wanted to know what was going on near that creek. I wanted to know why Shadow was there. What Shadow was. And I didn't want to go back by myself. This might be the only chance I'd have for a while to go with Quin. I spent so much time taking care of my father and brother — what was the harm in slipping out while Jack was sleeping?

"Well, maybe if we walk really fast," I said.

Quin was already on her feet.

"I'll leave a note," I added. "Not that he'll wake up, but still. I'll feel better."

I grabbed some paper and a pen from my dad's office and explained in huge block print that Quin and I were taking Henry on a quick walk to stretch his legs, and we'd be right back.

"What are you writing, a novel?" Quin said, sticking her head into the room. "Come on."

I left the note stuck to the refrigerator — the one place I was sure Jack would go first if he woke up. There was nothing to tape it up with so I wedged it into the handle, wishing Quin wouldn't rush me so much.

But at the same time I couldn't help feeling excited to finally be doing something for myself — something I wanted to do that didn't involve making dinner or keeping Jack company or any of the other things I did on a daily basis when Mom wasn't around to take care of them. Her job with the law firm was really important, and I was proud of her, but these days it seemed like she was away more than she was home. Sometimes I got tired of acting like an adult.

Right now, as I zipped up my fleece and pulled the front door quietly closed behind me, I knew I was definitely not acting grown-up. More like selfish and maybe even a little childish.

What surprised me was how good that felt.

6

"How can you not know? Either this is the place or it isn't," Quin said impatiently.

"I think it is," I said, looking back down the stretch of trail we'd just hiked over. "Almost. Maybe just two more minutes up the hill."

Henry was walking quietly by my side, which was a little unusual for him unless he was tired. But he didn't seem to be freaking out, or even just sensing anything unusual.

"That's what you said two minutes ago," Quin grumbled, thrusting her hands into her faded blue parka. She walked slightly ahead of me, her long, fat braid swinging from side to side.

She'd been getting progressively grumpier since we'd left the house. I was starting to rethink this whole plan.

"Wait," I cried, holding my hand up.

I could see a faint trail branching off to the right, sloping uphill.

"This is it," I said pointing. "This is where Henry took off. The first time that thing was around, it was just on the other side of that hill."

"Yeah?" Quin asked, her expression brightening. "So what are we waiting for?"

We both veered off onto the second path, trudging double time now that we knew we were almost there. She was slightly in front of me, and I practically had to jog to keep her from getting farther ahead.

When she reached the crest of the hill, Quin came to such an abrupt halt that I slammed into her and almost stepped on Henry.

"Oof," I said. "You could have —"

Quin shushed me. Then she pointed at a spot edged by low shrubs and vines, still coated with a morning frost.

It was the same place I'd found Henry cowering. I looked at my beagle. He was stock-still — almost rigid, but he didn't seem afraid now — and his eyes were locked on Quin. When I looked at her, I saw that she was returning the dog's gaze. It was almost like they were having a kind of conversation.

She might not be crazy, but this girl was definitely weird.

After a moment Quin leaned down and ran her hand over Henry's head, just once. His ears softened and his posture relaxed. Quin stood up, walked down the hill, glanced around, then fixed her gaze on a spot beyond a huge cluster of shrubs and willow bushes. She took several determined steps forward, pushing through the undergrowth, which seemed to simply close behind her, swallowing her so that she completely disappeared from view.

It was absolutely silent. Even the breeze seemed to fall away. I felt a chill creep up my spine.

"Quin?" I called.

Nothing.

I pulled Henry forward, catching my boot on a tangle of brush and feeling the painful twinge of a muscle pull.

"Quin?" I called again.

I could hear nothing but the sound of branches scraping against my jeans as I forced my way through the bushes as Quin had done. Henry had less trouble, since he was closer to the ground, but the leash kept getting tangled. The more I pushed forward, the thicker the tangle of branches and undergrowth seemed to become. Where in the world had Quin gone?

Feeling panic rise in my throat, I pushed forward twice as hard, ignoring the sharp branches poking at my legs and slapping at my arms. The leash caught on something and I tugged it free. All I seemed to be doing was working myself deeper into what felt like an enormous snare of roots and limbs and leaves. I felt as if the branches were grabbing me, clutching at me even as I shoved them away. I was just about to scream Quin's name at the top of my lungs when Henry and I pushed free of the mesh of plants and stumbled forward into a clearing.

Poking out of the trees that encircled the clearing was a rotting old structure — something that once, a very long time ago, might have been a cabin. Quin was standing several feet away from it. I almost yelled with relief at the sight of her.

"Didn't you hear me calling you? You just disappeared — I was scared!" I exclaimed.

She didn't answer me. She didn't even turn around to look at me. She just stood there, staring at a dark hole in the front of the cabin that appeared to be the remains of a doorway. Something about the way she looked, like she was in some kind of a trance, unnerved me. I marched over, pulling my reluctant beagle along, and grabbed her arm.

"Quin!"

She turned her face toward me, and I had just enough time to register how pale her skin had grown under cold-flushed cheeks when I heard a low, dangerous growl.

Now I understood why Quin had frozen. I cinched Henry's leash absolutely tight, so that he couldn't move even an inch from me. Anyone who spent time hiking would instinctively stop moving when they heard that sound. Rule number one, stay still. Rule number two, figure out where it is, and what it is. If it is a bear, make a lot of noise and move off. If it is a wolf . . . We didn't have wolves back home. I had no idea what I was supposed to do if I crossed paths with one.

The growl came again, deep and menacing. My eyes followed the sound, and suddenly I found the source, a low dark shape in the remains of the cabin doorway. My heart started pounding as I caught the glimpse of fur and paws. This was no Shadow. I could see it now. Definitely a wolf.

"Easy, boy," Quin said, taking a small, slow step forward.

Was she nuts? Who in their right mind would try to sweet-talk a wolf?

"Quin, no," I tried to say, but no sound came out at all.

60

"Easy," she said again, taking a second small step forward.

There was a terrible snarl and I braced for the shock of the thing launching itself at Quin's throat. We were both dead, that much was clear.

But the wolf stayed where it was, in the doorway. It snarled again. As my eyes adapted to the darkness beyond the cabin's entrance, I could see the animal was baring its teeth, eyes blazing and ears flattened in an unmistakable threat. But still the wolf did not attack Quin. I could see now that the animal's eyes were pale blue, and its face black. Its head was up and its chest barrel-shaped. I could also make out a tail, curled over its back. I realized all at once I had made a mistake. This was no wolf.

"It's a dog," I whispered.

This was not necessarily good news. It was a dog, yes. But a huge, angry, snarling dog in the middle of nowhere. We were probably still dead.

"Easy, boy," Quin murmured, taking another clearly suicidal step toward the animal.

The dog, who had been standing, sat down in the center of the doorway.

"That's better," Quin said quietly. "It's okay, boy. We're friends."

"Just be careful," I whispered.

Quin extended one hand toward the dog, which definitely did not qualify as being careful as far as I was concerned. His ears flattened slightly, and he got to his feet again. She pulled her hand back a little, turned it palm up, and let it hover there. I hung on to Henry with all my might, but there was no need. He was pressing into my leg, his head down, his body in the submissive position he took whenever there was clearly an alpha dog around.

The huge dog's ears came forward again, and his tail began to wag very slightly.

"He likes you," I said, wondering again why Quin seemed to have such a strange power over dogs.

"Or he's hungry," Quin replied.

The dog wagged his tail again, a small wag. Quin extended her hand just a bit closer, her eyes on his. I thought she was pushing her luck now. Something was going to give. Henry was going to bark or the dog was going to pounce. But neither of those things happened. Without warning, the dog turned and retreated into the cabin. In a flash, Quin went in after him, disappearing into the dark interior.

Here we go again, I thought. I wasn't sure if Quin was really brave, really stupid, or both. But I'd followed her this far, and her instincts seemed good. Feeling around in my side pocket for the little flashlight I always carried, I went through the doorway after her, still keeping Henry on a tight leash. He resisted a little this time, clearly not too keen on the idea of going into this gloomy place.

It was dark and freezing cold inside the ruined building. The air felt damp and smelled of wood, mildew and decaying leaves. I could just make out Quin in front of me. Henry pressed tight against my leg, trembling slightly. I switched the flashlight on and Quin jumped slightly as the space was filled with light.

"Flashlight," Quin said. "Nice thinking."

"Never hurts to be prepared," I said. I shone the light in a circle around us. The walls of the cabin were more or less intact, but there was a pile of rubble in the back where part of the roof had caved in. I looked up. The framework remained and was almost entirely covered with vines, but through the leaves I could see glimpses of the sky.

"Do you see him?" Quin asked.

I trained the light on one corner, then carefully swept it in an arc around the entire perimeter.

"Is he behind the pile of junk?" I asked.

"Here, boy! Come on, boy!" Quin called, walking over to what was left of the roof. I walked over to the pile of rubble and stood next to her. "He's not back there," Quin said.

At that moment, we heard a low, sinister snarling. I couldn't see the animal anywhere, but I knew dogs well enough to know that this snarl meant business. We were being warned away. We were being threatened. This was an animal who wanted us to leave, or we would be attacked.

"Where is it?" Quin whispered, frozen in place.

The snarl grew higher, uglier. I could imagine the black dog with his teeth bared and his pale blue eyes blazing. I was scared, and something about the air seemed to go strange, as if it was charged with electricity.

"We need to get out of here now," I whispered back, holding Henry's leash absolutely tight so he could not move an inch. Quin nodded, just barely.

Our arms pressed against each other, we slowly and carefully backed out of the cabin, pulling Henry along — though the beagle was only too happy to get outside. The moment we passed through the old door, the snarling stopped. Almost as if someone had hit a mute button.

Just to be safe, we put another twenty feet or so between ourselves and the cabin door.

"I don't think he's coming after us," Quin said.

"That was really scary," I told her.

Quin was watching the cabin with a worried expression.

"I wonder . . . what was up with that? What was he so protective of?" she asked.

"I don't know," I said. "But I do know that I kind of want to get out of here, pronto."

Quin looked at me like she'd just remembered something. "How are we for time?"

I pulled up my sleeve so I could read my watch, and exclaimed with dismay.

"Uh-oh. It's ten of eleven," I said. "We've got to get back to Jack."

Quin shot one more look in the direction of the cabin, her eyebrows furrowed. Then she adjusted her pack on her shoulders and nudged me.

"We can make it in twenty minutes," Quin said, pushing past me. "But I hope you like running,"

"I hate it," I said.

Nonetheless, with visions of a hysterical Jack filling my head, I matched Quin's steady jog, trying to talk and catch my breath at the same time.

"I really thought that dog was going to attack us," I said. "But I'm thinking now he was just really afraid of something. He was obviously cold and hungry. I just feel so bad leaving him like that. If we could have gotten a little closer, maybe I could have looped my scarf around, used it as a leash."

"What are you talking about?" Quin asked. She was nowhere near as out of breath as I was. I was a hiker, not a jogger. I slowed us down to a fast walk, which Henry also clearly preferred, now that we'd put a good distance between us and the mystery dog.

"Well, to bring him back, find out who he belongs to," I said. "Give him something to eat. Call the humane society, something."

Quin stopped and took my arm.

"Tee, there is no owner," she said.

"How can you possibly know that?" I asked.

"Didn't you feel it?" she asked. "Don't you see?"

I stared at my new friend, waiting, realizing as she began to speak that I already knew.

"That wasn't anybody's lost dog. That was Shadow."

DODIE

Caspian dropped to the ground after Daddy hit him with the stick, like everything had gone out of him, like he remembered where he was and who he was again.

Silla and I tried to go to Caspian, but Daddy wouldn't let us. Finally he let Vernon, one of our best dog handlers, treat Caspian's wound. Then Daddy made Vernon lock Caspian up in a pen by himself. If Silla had not been crying and begging so hard, I think Daddy would have been done with Caspian right there and then. Jim was badly bitten, and my father believed that a dog who had bitten a human once could never be trusted to work a team with other dogs or humans.

But Caspian was our heart dog. Silla and I loved him as fiercely as we loved each other. And Daddy would listen if Silla begged him for something very hard. He loved her more than he loved the rest of us, and she was *the youngest and the prettiest so we all loved her too and didn't mind. Because Silla pleaded, Daddy let Caspian stay in the kennel. After his wound healed, Caspian was even let back with the other pups. Caspian grew into a fine, powerful young dog.*

Still, Silla and I both knew that Daddy never trusted him, especially around Silla, who had always been small and fragile, prone to terrible chest colds and other ailments that often made it difficult for her to breathe. She was delicate, it was true. But Caspian would never have hurt her. He would not have hurt anyone. Though I could not prove it, I believe it was Caspian who saved the pups that night. Vernon had found the tracks of a single wolf circling the kennel. Silla and I believed that the wind blew open the unlatched door to the pups' pen and the wolf crept in during the night. Then, we were sure, Caspian had charged that wolf to lead it away from his terrified brothers and sisters.

Of this we had no proof, but it was what we felt. It was what we read on the wind. It was what we knew in our hearts had happened that night.

7

Jack was standing in the hallway when we came through the front door. His hair was poking out in three distinct directions, and the imprint of his pillow was still clear on one side of his face.

"Where were you?" he asked sleepily.

"Just taking Henry for a little walk," I said, trying to disguise the huffing and puffing I was doing after the fast march all the way back to the house.

"What do you look so weird for, then?" Jack asked.

"Who's calling who weird?" Quin said, stepping around to stand next to me and giving my brother a long, appraising look. "Let's see — Batman pajamas, wind-tunnel hair, a drool trail on both sides of the mouth — I'm thinking *you're* the one that looks weird."

Jack's mouth hung open, and he seemed frankly astonished

to see Quin standing there. He decided to pretend she did not exist.

"Do we have Cap'n Crunch?" he asked me.

"We had two boxes yesterday, and no one else in this house would actually eat the stuff," I said.

"'Cause you're stupidy-dumb," Jack told me, darting toward the kitchen.

"Stupidy-dumb, huh? Impressive vocabulary," Quin said. "How proud you must be, Tee."

I grinned at her.

"You have no idea," I replied. Lowering my voice, I added, "I don't think he realized we were gone."

I heard the sound of a spoon and a plastic bowl hitting the kitchen floor and bouncing. I rolled my eyes.

"Let me just go get him set up with his cereal," I said. "My room's right in there — we can hang out. I'll get us some juice."

"Okay," Quin said easily, unzipping her fleece as she walked into the room I had pointed to.

Jack had abandoned the bowl and spoon where they fell and was sitting at the table eating Cap'n Crunch by the handful out of the box, reading an old He-Man comic book. He barely seemed to notice me as I placed the bowl and spoon on the table, filled the bowl with cereal, and poured milk over it. When I handed him the spoon he scooped up a heap of cereal and crammed it into his mouth, his eyes still never leaving the comic book.

"What do you say?" I asked, grabbing the pitcher of juice and a couple glasses.

"Thapp yuh," Jack said as politely as he could with his mouth full.

"You're welcome," I replied. "Quin and I are going to hang out in my room for a while. You and I need to get online and check what work you have to do after. At least do some of the long-division stuff. One hour, okay?"

Jack nodded and gave me a little wave, which probably meant he hadn't actually listened to what I was saying. Fine with me. We had one thing in common — neither one of us wanted to deal with third-grade long-division assignments via the Internet.

When I walked into my room, Quin was standing by the shelf where I'd unpacked all the books I'd brought with me, her head tilted to one side as she scanned the titles. I was dying to get back to talking about Shadow now that I wasn't huffing and puffing, but seeing Quin there made me realize why I felt like I knew her. She reminded me of myself, in many ways. For example, if I went to someone's house and noticed a bookshelf, I did exactly the same thing.

"The vampire book was a gift — don't hold it against me," I said, setting the glasses of juice down and sitting on the edge of my bed.

Quin turned and gave me a mischievous grin that said she was already holding it against me.

"Suuuuurrrre," she said. "And you're just holding this *Zodiac Guide to Besties and Boys* for a friend, right?"

I smacked my hands over my face and flopped backward on my bed.

"That one's mine. I like the quizzes, okay?"

"I love astrology quizzes," Quin said, plopping down next to me. "Let's do me. I'm a Libra."

I sat up.

"So am I!" I said.

"Look at us — we're living *The Parent Trap*," Quin said. "In about a week of comparing notes we'll realize that we're identical twins who were separated at birth."

"Except you're tall and have red hair, and I'm short and have black hair," I pointed out.

"Excuse me, but I have *strawberry blonde* hair and I'm considered medium height," Quin said. "And you aren't short."

"I'm shortish," I said.

"Petite," Quin corrected, flipping through the book.

" 'Question one. On your ideal date, would you most enjoy (a) a dinner at a trendy new restaurant, (b) a long walk on the beach, or (c) a burger and an evening of bowling?' That's it? Those are my only choices?"

"I choose (d) spinsterhood," I said.

"Right," Quin agreed. "Or (e) browsing the stacks at Barnes & Noble."

"Plus, we need to know who the date is with," I said. "Bowling can be dangerous if your partner has terrible aim."

"And we need to know what state we live in," Quin added. "Is this beach we might walk on in Malibu or Maine?"

"Yeah, and this hypothetical burger at the bowling alley . . . I mean, does it come with fries or anything? Can I get a milkshake?"

"Definitely not enough information," Quin said. "Let's move on to question two. 'When you and a boyfriend call it quits, do you prefer to (a) stay friends, (b) never speak again, or (c) take a break then try to hang out after things have cooled down?' Wait, we're calling it quits already? After one lousy burger? That's so harsh!"

"Boys stink," I declared.

" 'Question three. You meet your dream guy at last, and he's perfect in every way. Except for one. You have a dog, and he is allergic to them. Do you (a) try to find another home for your dog, (b) work night and day vacuuming to keep the allergens to a minimum, or (c) break up with your dream guy?'"

"Break up with the dream guy," we both said in unison.

Quin slammed the book closed.

"What a question, even. Who's going to choose some guy over her dog? Seriously?"

"I know," I agreed. "If you farm your dog out just so you can have a boyfriend, you didn't deserve the dog in the first place."

"Exactly," Quin declared. "I prefer most dogs to people, to be honest. Gatsby was all the best friend I needed."

"Gatsby?" I asked.

Quin's face clouded. "Yeah. He was my dog — a German shepherd. He got loose last year, took off. He was hit by a car before we even knew he was missing."

Tears filled my eyes.

"Oh, Quin, I'm so, so sorry," I said.

She waved her hand in the air in a let's-not-talk-about-it gesture.

"Anyway, enough of this book," she said, tossing it aside.

"Totally," I said. "Now . . . I mean, do you feel like doing something else? What would you normally be doing if you weren't here?"

I wanted to ask her a million questions about Shadow. How she knew he wasn't just another dog, when he looked like one — when I could see him there, plain as day. But she had clammed up on the walk home, and I wanted to be careful. I was really getting to like Quin, and I didn't want to blow it.

"Reading," Quin said. "Hiking."

Only my two favorite things to do, in that order. I sat up and stared at her. She was lying on the bed with her feet propped up against the wall.

"Seriously, Quin, you're like . . . me. But in a different body. It's a little freaky."

"I know — I've noticed it too," Quin said. "I almost never meet anybody my age I can stand at all. How long are you staying in Alaska?"

"Two weeks — at least, that's what our dad told the school to get permission to pull us out. In reality, though, it all depends on when he feels like he's got enough done on the book. I suppose it's possible we could end up leaving before that, but I don't think that's going to happen. He's in this major writer's-block place right now. He's waiting for the lightning bolt of inspiration to hit him."

Quin began to peel one of her socks off using her other foot as leverage.

"Doesn't sound so bad, if you don't mind total unpredictability," Quin said. "Where do you actually live, anyway?"

"At the moment? Woodstock, in upstate New York. Before that, Vermont. And before that, Cape Cod. My mom is a lawyer, and companies hire her for specific jobs, so she doesn't have to live near some main office. This past year she's been traveling a ton. And Dad's obsessed with finding the perfect writers' town."

Quin started in on removing her other sock.

"My parents split," she said. "Six years ago. My mom hated living here, hated everything about Alaska. Finally ditched Nome, and us along with it, for New York City."

"That's terrible," I said.

"I guess," Quin replied quietly. "It's better this way, just me and Dad. We understand each other."

We lay on the bed together in silence for a few moments, Quin examining her feet. I could tell she didn't want to talk about her parents, and I couldn't leave the other question unasked any longer.

"Quin, how did you know that was Shadow?" I asked. "It's not that I don't believe you. I'm actually *sure* you're right. I just didn't know until you said it. Did you see something I didn't?"

Quin pulled the elastic band from her hair, unbraided her ponytail, and began rebraiding it before answering me.

"Well, it's not so much what I saw, it's more what I could feel. I've always had a really good way with all animals, but especially dogs. When I'm around a dog I sort of pick up what they're feeling and what their temperament is. I got it right away from your beagle — that first day I came here and you got back from the walk with him. I knew he'd had a scare. And when I'm getting this kind of feeling thing from a dog, something happens where it seems like the dog *knows* it. In some way, it's like we're communicating."

Quin looked at me, as if she still thought I was going to accuse her of being nuts. I nodded, though, hoping she'd go on, and after a moment, she did.

"But that dog this morning? There was nothing there that I could feel. Not in the way I usually do. It might as well have been a hologram or something. The really weird thing is that when I realized that, I sort of adapted. I started picking up on the dog anyway. And I could see he was picking up on me. He was interested in Henry first, though, because who gets a dog better than another dog?"

I rolled over onto my stomach and propped my chin on my hands, in the same position Quin was now in.

"That makes sense," I said. "And Henry sort of adapted

also. He was really scared that first day. But the second time we were near Shadow, he was more . . . expectant. And today, he didn't seem scared of Shadow until the snarling started, and then we were all scared. Yeah, it all fits now. It's amazing — I've never heard of a dog ghost."

"Well, if people can be ghosts, why couldn't dogs?" Quin asked. "Doesn't it ever irritate you the way humans always assume that they're so above every other form of life? I had this teacher once who I ran into when I was walking Clancy — he was our dog when I was little. And she said something along the lines of 'what an expressive face — it's almost like he's thinking something.' Why would anyone assume that dogs don't think and feel and dream and do everything we do, and probably more?"

"I know what you mean," I said. "Like when scientists say they might have proof that dolphins are communicating with each other. There needs to be proof of that, like it's some wackadoodle Life on Mars theory?" I paused. "What would make a dog haunt a place, though?"

Quin slipped one of her socks onto her hands, then pulled it off and rolled it into a little ball.

"Whatever the usual people reasons would be," Quin mused. "Something bad happened there. Or unfinished business. Or a warning."

I thought of the dog ghost's face — the dark fur and strangely pale blue eyes — the strength evident in his barrel chest and powerful legs. Poor thing. What could have happened to him?

"I wonder how old that cabin is," I said. "And why someone would have built a cabin smack in the middle of nowhere."

"It isn't really in the middle of nowhere, not by Alaska standards," Quin said. "That trail goes up toward Dorothy Creek, where miners were panning for gold. There could easily be any number of abandoned miner's cabins out there."

"When was that?" I asked.

"The gold rush started at the very end of the 1800s," Quin told me. "There's just no way to know when that particular cabin was built, though. Like I said, there are abandoned ones all over the place."

"If we went back and really looked, maybe we could find something in all that rubble with a date on it. Or even a name."

Quin started unraveling her braid again, her blue eyes on mine. I noticed the smattering of freckles on her nose and cheeks for the first time.

"What's so important about finding out who built the cabin when?" she asked.

"Well, if we found that out, we might be able to learn something about the dog. I don't know, maybe we could help him or something. Like that TV show where the girl helps ghosts understand they're dead so they can move on."

"*Ghost Whisperer* meets the *Dog Whisperer*," Quin said. I laughed.

"Exactly. We'd be dog-ghost whisperers."

"How would we help a dog ghost, though?" she asked.

"I don't know," I said, truthfully. "But the thing is, I think you're totally right that Shadow picked up on Henry first, but then he sensed you. When you spoke to him, put your hand out — he stopped growling. He relaxed a little. And he was looking right at you. He didn't get aggressive again until we walked inside that cabin. Didn't you get the feeling Shadow is asking for help?"

"Yeah, I did," Quin said. "He definitely wants something or needs something, and it's really important. I felt it. I don't even know where to start, but we've got to find a way to help that dog."

"Help what dog?"

Jack was standing in the doorway, still in his pajamas. One tiny golden nugget of Cap'n Crunch was stuck to the bottom of his lip.

"We were just talking about a TV show," I said quickly. Helping Shadow meant making a trip back to the old cabin, and the last thing we needed was to have Jack invite himself to that expedition.

"No you weren't," Jack countered. "You found a dog, and I want to see it."

"Well you can't," Quin said. "It's a secret."

"No it isn't," Jack said.

I sighed with exasperation. "Yes it is, Jack. Quin and I were having a private conversation, and you aren't allowed to eavesdrop. It's against the rules."

"If you don't tell me about the dog, then I'll tell Dad," Jack said.

"You'll tell Dad I have a secret dog?" I asked with a laugh. "Fine, go right ahead."

"Not that," Jack said. He pressed his lips into a grim little line, and the morsel of cereal dropped off onto his shirt. "I'll tell him about this morning."

"What about this morning?" I asked, narrowing my eyes.

"About you and her going off exploring and leaving me alone," Jack said. "That's against the rules too, and you know it. Mom told Dad he could count on you, but he can't now."

My face flushed red. Jack sure knew how to get me.

It wasn't like my father would hand down some heavy-duty punishment if he found out I'd left Jack unattended. He wasn't like that. He'd just be . . . disappointed. That was worse than anything. I felt a wave of anger toward my little brother.

"Just try it," I said in a low voice. "Find out what happens. Because I'm still going to be in charge of you while we're here. I'll have you doing math all day long, and you can kiss that Nintendo DS goodbye."

Jack's lower lip quivered, and he balled his hands up into little fists.

"Hey, guys, cool off," Quin said, getting up from the bed and walking over to Jack. "It's no big deal. Yeah, Jack — you're right. We went out this morning — my fault. I talked Tee into it. And yeah, we saw a dog out there. We don't know much more than that, right now. It's kind of a boring story."

Jack beamed at Quin, and sat down on the edge of a small wooden trunk by the door. His lips had stopped quivering. Quin might not think she could read people, but she just had. All Jack ever really wanted was to be included.

"I want to hear it anyway," he said. "The whole story."

Quin sat down next to him.

"Okay, well, for starters, have you ever heard of a dog-ghost whisperer?"

Jack shook his head, his eyes huge.

"Well, neither had we, before we took a walk out in those woods, but we were kind of scared anyway. Some people say there's a witch living out there, you know. Other people say there's a strange, smoky shadow that creeps up on you and watches you while you walk. But what we found was an old, falling-down cabin."

Jack was staring at Quin intently, his mouth slightly open, hanging on her every word.

Quin glanced in my direction, gave me a wink, then turned back toward Jack and began to explain how we'd found a dog in an old cabin in the woods. I curled up and closed my eyes, focusing on the sound of Quin's voice. She described everything so vividly that an image sprang into my mind's eye as clearly as if I were seeing it again — the face of a dog with pale, haunting blue eyes.

8

I don't know who invented the term *cabin fever*, but I definitely had it. After Quin went home with her father, I'd spent most of that evening helping Jack with his assignments while Dad worked. Today had been equally dull — Dad holed up in his office, and me juggling entertaining my little brother, doing my own school assignments, and taking Henry out for the occasional breather. So when Dad emerged to tell us that we were invited to Joe's house for dinner, I almost yelled with excitement. I'd get out of the house *and* be able to spend the evening with Quin — it was perfect.

But there was another whole hour to kill before it would be time to go. And I felt if I did not get out of the house that moment, I was going to go stark raving bonkers.

"Henry, walkies!" I called.

Henry trotted down the hall to where I was standing, wagging his tail but looking slightly suspicious. He'd been on two walks already, and he didn't seem sure about a third.

"Come on, buddy," I told him, kneeling down to rub his silky ears. Henry sighed, then plummeted onto his back, paws in the air, offering me his round white belly.

"Nope," I told him sternly. "Get up. You and I both need to get out of here."

"Me too," I heard. I looked up at Jack, who looked small and forlorn, a smudge of orange highlighter on one cheek.

"You finished reviewing your vocabulary work sheet?" I asked him.

Jack nodded, looking so glum I knew he was telling the truth.

"I was just going to go up the trail as far as the rise," I said. "It's cold, and there really isn't time to go farther."

"Good," Jack said, already tired of the walk we hadn't started yet. I guess he had cabin fever as bad as I did.

"Bundle up," I told him, grabbing at the pile of warm things now lying in a heap by the door.

"I am," he protested.

It was a good ten minutes before Jack was ready, layered up so he was as round as a snowman. The Nordic cap, price tag still dangling off the back, topped off the look.

Henry waited patiently while I clipped his leash on. He

definitely wasn't all that interested in more exercise. None of us were. We went outside and started slowly up the usual trail, taking our time. The only point, really, was to have something to do until it would finally be time to go to Quin's house.

"It's cold," Jack complained.

Usually Jack's griping really irritated me. But today, I was right there with him.

"I know, right? It's spring! Can you imagine what January is like around here?"

"And there's nowhere to skateboard," he added.

"Nope," I agreed. "But you don't skateboard, Jackster."

"If I wanted to learn, though, I couldn't," Jack said. "It's not fair."

"When you put it that way, I guess it's not," I told him.

We trudged quietly for a moment.

"Tee? Is there really a dog ghost, or did Quin make it up?"

"She didn't make it up," I said. "She believes there's a dog ghost, and so do I. I guess we could be wrong, though."

"Do dogs go the same place as people when they die?" he asked.

"I don't know."

"Is everyone a ghost, or can they decide not to be?" he pressed.

"I don't know," I said again.

Another few moments passed, then Jack asked, "If there are ghosts, can they watch us all the time?"

"I figure even ghosts must have better things to do than that," I told him, forcing a cheerful note into my voice. Really, his questions were kind of giving me the creeps.

"What if a ghost gets mad at you? What if it decides to follow you everywhere you go and never leave you alone?"

"Jack, that's ridiculous," I said, more sharply than I meant to.

"Is there really a witch living out there?" he asked.

"I don't think so," I said. "Anyway, there's no such thing as witches."

I believed that. About ghosts, I was definitely not so sure.

My little brother finally fell silent for a few moments. And then he changed the subject, thankfully.

"Do you think Quin might have a popcorn maker at her house?" he asked. "And if she does, do you think she'd let us make it, and melt real butter in a saucepan like Mom does and pour it on top?"

My stomach rumbled and my feet were like blocks of ice and I felt a sudden, gnawing craving for hot buttered popcorn.

"That would hit the spot," I said. "Here's hoping."

We had reached the top of the rise, where we paused. I looked around at the landscape, hilly with increasing undergrowth ahead to the north, back in the direction of home. Though it was late afternoon, the sun was high in the sky. Spring sunset in Nome was not until ten o'clock. It was another thing that was hard to get used to — it just threw everything off.

In the distance, I heard a low, long, quavering howl. Jack froze, his eyes huge and his mouth open in a small frightened O. The howl came again. Henry stood up, ears pricked, his tail quivering as he listened.

"Is that him, Tee? Is that the dog ghost?" Jack asked, his face tight with fear.

"I think it is," I told him truthfully.

"Can we go home right now?" he pressed anxiously.

I put my arm around my little brother.

"Yeah," I told him. "We can."

I stared out the window at the center of Nome as we drove down Front Street. The buildings were low and close together, most only one or two stories high. Telephone wires crisscrossed overhead, strung from tall, T-shaped telephone poles. The street was wide, and the whole town had a sort of frontier feeling to it, like we'd wandered onto the set of a Wild West movie.

"This is it," my dad said, pulling over and parking in front of a house.

"Cool!" yelled Jack. "Look how close the other houses are — you could pass secret messages through the windows!"

I got out of the car and looked at the house curiously. Quin's home was a simple one-story wooden structure with a peaked roof. The wood siding was unpainted and looked fairly old, giving the house the weather-beaten-but-cozy look of so many of the little beach houses I'd seen when we lived on Cape Cod. An oversized mailbox by the front walkway read, *The Hendersons*.

"Let's go," Dad said.

Jack shot up the walk ahead of us, my father and I taking a more dignified pace behind him.

"Long, boring day, huh?" he asked, ruffling my hair.

"No, not at all," I said. "It was fine. Maybe a little slow, yeah. I don't mind, though."

"I don't mean to keep throwing you together with Quin," he said. "I know you like your alone time, and Joe said Quin isn't always the most sociable person, either."

"Actually, Dad, she's great!" I said, as we reached the front door. "I really like her."

My father gave me a look of genuine surprise.

"Wow. She must really be something special," he said.

"She is," I said.

There was no doorbell, so I knocked on the door loudly. Seconds later, Joe opened it.

"Beckett!" he said. "Tee, Jack — you made it! Come on in before you freeze to death."

We walked into the main room of the house — a cozy living room and kitchen all in one. Every available space on the wall was filled with crammed bookshelves. An oversized couch and mismatched armchair occupied the corner farthest from the kitchen. Between them was a massive wood-burning stove. Quin was lying on the floor beside it, an open book on the rug in front of her. She turned when I came in, and her serious expression was instantly replaced by a smile.

"Finally!" she said. She patted the spot next to her and I flopped down, loving the feel of the heat and the scent of burning wood.

"Wow, check it out!" Jack yelled, making a beeline for the stove and almost stepping on my head in the process. "This is so cool! It's like the thing the witch tried to push Hansel and Gretel into. How come it's so much bigger than ours? Do these ever explode? If they did, would we all die?"

Joe's response was to hand Jack a steaming mug. He placed another next to me. Hot chocolate. It tasted like heaven. Even better than hot buttered popcorn.

"Thanks," I said.

"Hope you're hungry, 'cause this is just about ready," Joe said, stirring something in a large pot on the stove.

Now, there was one difference between Quin and me. In my family, Dad never did the cooking.

"Starving," my father said. "I think I forgot to eat today. I'm missing something, Joe, and if I could just find it I could really get this book going. I've gone through the papers, the letters, the newspaper articles, everything the archives have, but the idea of humans and dogs working and living together in reality — firsthand accounts — it still needs that. I need to talk to somebody myself."

"Clay might have an idea or two," Joe said, replacing the lid on the pot. "He ought to be here any minute now."

"I hate clay," Jack said. "They made us make stuff with it in art last year, and everything I made looked all squished on one side."

"Clay's a person," Quin told Jack. I lifted an eyebrow at her. A person?

"He's really cool," Quin whispered to me. "The best. He was, like, my savior when I lost Gatsby. You'll love him."

I hadn't realized anyone else was coming to dinner, let alone a cool guy. I was dressed super casually in fleece-lined jeans and an enormous wool fisherman's sweater. Not that I cared about boys, or anything. But still. The sound of knocking put an end to any possibility of switching my sweater for something better fitting of Quin's. The really cool boy had arrived.

"Clay, this is Beckett and his children, Tee and Jack."

I blinked in surprise as I sat up. Clay was no boy. His hair was snow white, with a matching walrus moustache. His face was deeply lined, but his bright blue eyes were young and glittering. For no reason I could explain, I immediately liked him.

"Are you Quin's grandpa?" Jack asked.

"Jack, don't be rude," I hissed. Although I wasn't exactly sure how rude it was. Clay certainly looked old enough to be somebody's grandpa, and surely he was aware of that.

Clay laughed, a deep growly sound that made me want to laugh too.

"When they start lettin' me pick my grandkids, I expect Quin'll be the first on my list," he said to Jack.

"I better be the *only* one on your list," Quin said, getting up. She gave Clay a kiss on the cheek, and beamed when he ruffled her hair.

"Okay, troops, let's dig in," Joe said.

A round wooden table near the kitchen had been set for six. Within moments we were all seated and Joe was ladling hot fish stew into each of our bowls as Quin passed around a basket heaped with fat slices of bread.

"Well, Clay, Joe says you know a great deal about dog teams and mushers — I'd really love it if you'd let me interview you," my father said, covering a piece of bread with what looked like about an inch of butter.

I looked from Clay to Quin, then back to Clay.

"I'm glad to, though I don't know how much help I'll be. I know a little. But the one person that knows more about dogs, and dogs with people, that's Dorothy Shaktoolik. But I guess she don't talk to nobody, not these days anyway."

"Clay knows dogs as well as anyone in Alaska. He finished the Iditarod seven times," Quin said, with obvious pride. "And he placed in the top three twice."

"Whoa," Jack said, dropping his spoon with a clatter as his eyes grew huge. "You were in the Iditarod? The huge dog-racing thing?"

Clay gave Jack a shy smile.

"Well, I guess I was, Jack," he said. "A long time ago. And that's a good way to describe it. It sure was a huge dog-racing thing."

"When were you in it? How fast do the dogs go? Do wolves eat any of the mushers? How come they call it the Iditarod?"

Clay laughed his growly laugh.

"Might as well start with the last question first. Iditarod's the name of an old mining town. The dog trail went through it, so they started calling it the Iditarod trail. Name stuck."

"But how come the mushers race it?" Jack pressed.

"Because of Balto," Quin said. Jack gave her a blank look. "What? Everybody knows who Balto is."

"No, they don't," Jack argued. Which meant that he didn't.

"Balto was a sled dog," Dad said. "He was . . . see, there was a terrible epidemic of diphtheria in Nome. Kind of like the flu, but much, much worse. This was around, what, 1924?"

"1925," Joe said.

"Right," Dad agreed. "And there were no roads into Nome in those days. In the winter, you couldn't get there by boat because of the ice. Most planes couldn't fly in those conditions back then. There was a train that went up to Nenana, but that was more than six hundred miles away. Whole families were falling sick — people were dying — and there was no way to get medicine to them. The whole town was frozen in."

"Then somebody came up with the idea of using the dog teams that did the mail runs," Clay said. "Back in those days a sled and a good dog team was the only reliable way to get around. That's how they delivered the mail. So each town along the line got in touch with the others on the telegraph machine, and they arranged for mushers and dogs to be waiting at every town along the mail route. The first team picked up crates of medicine in Nenana, and it went from one team to the next."

"Like a relay race?" Jack asked.

Clay pointed at Jack like he'd said something brilliant. "That's exactly what it was. Those mushers and teams worked day and night to get that medicine through, and they did it. Got it into Nome just six days after loading it up in Nenana. Saved a lot of lives. And the Iditarod follows most of the trail those teams took, to keep their memory alive."

"But what about Balto? What did he do?" Jack asked.

"His team got lost in a blizzard," Quin said, "and the lead dog couldn't find the way back to the trail. The musher put Balto up front to give him a try at leading, and Balto found the trail and got the medicine into Nome."

"Whoa," Jack said again. "That's so cool. So he, like, saved a whole town."

"Well, Balto's the one that got famous for it, that's true," Clay said, stirring his stew. "But there were twenty teams that ran themselves ragged on the trail, and every single one of them deserved equal credit. Balto was one heck of an animal, no doubt about it. But it could have been any one of them lead dogs that pulled that sled into Nome. All those reporters and photographers, they all did their stories just about Balto. 'Hero dog,' all the papers called him. Took him all across the country on a tour. Even had statues built of him. There was some bad feeling about that in Nome for a long time. Plenty of mushers felt like their dog teams didn't get their due. When the Iditarod comes each year, we remember all those dogs."

"You must have some stories," my father said.

Clay chuckled and dunked a piece of bread into his bowl, mopping up the last of the fish stew.

"I guess I do," he said. "Which reminds me, I brought a whole folder full of pictures of sled dogs. Nice pictures — going all the way back to before the race. I think a few of 'em are older than I am."

"Oh, can I see them?" Quin asked. "I'm done eating."

"They're in a bag by the front door," Clay said.

Quin gave her father a pleading look. "Dad? Can I be excused — can Tee and I go look at the pictures?"

"Sure," Joe said. "Wash your hands first — don't want to get fish stew on them."

"What about me?" Jack complained as Quin and I stood up.

"Jack, ask Clay to tell you about the time he and his dogs went missing in the blizzard of 1991," Quin said.

Jack's mouth dropped open, and he forgot all about the dog pictures.

"What happened? Did you almost die? Can your toes really fall off if they get too cold? If they do, can you just stick them back on?"

Quin and I headed out of the room, though part of me really wanted to stay and hear Clay talk about being lost in the blizzard with his dogs.

"Here it is," Quin said, picking up a shopping bag by the door. "Let's go to my room. It's up there."

Quin was pointing at a ladder, which I realized I had walked right past without noticing. It was built into the wall, and it led to a large loft area above the main floor. I climbed up behind Quin.

"Wow," I said. The loft was amazing. It was just as big as my bedroom back in Woodstock, with a low double bed, a beanbag chair, several good lamps, and rows and rows of bookshelves. "This is fabulous," I told her.

"It's pretty cozy," she admitted. She flopped onto the bed, holding the fat folder of pictures, and I did the same.

The first picture Quin pulled out was a color photo of a hefty-looking dog with distinct markings on his face. He was mostly black, with a mask of white on his muzzle and around his eyes, and a jet-black stripe up the center of his nose. Quin turned the photo over.

"It says this is Piccalo," she read. "Iditarod runner — doesn't say the year."

She pulled out the next picture.

A dog with a mottled coat was standing with another dog, his face turned toward the camera. He was wearing a red harness and little racing booties on each paw. The fur around his muzzle and eyes looked almost gray, giving him the appearance of an old man. The tip of one of his ears drooped slightly. But you could see by the way he was standing that he was a powerful, fast dog.

"Zorro," Quin read. "Owned by four-time winner Lance Mackey — oh, I know who he is. The Mackeys are super-famous here. They have a kennel."

I pulled a picture from the file. It was an old black-and-white shot, the edges yellowed with age. A somber-faced man in a heavy dark jacket stared into the camera, an enormous pure white dog in his arms. The dog's head was tilted back and his nose was touching the man's face, almost as if he were giving the man a kiss. I turned the photo over.

"Leonhard Seppala with Vodka, 1936," I read.

"Let me see," Quin said. I pushed the picture to her.

"Beautiful," she said. "Here's another really old one."

We stared at the black-and-white portrait. The dog was dark brown or black, powerfully built, with ears that stood straight up and pale, intelligent eyes.

I knew that face.

"Whoa," Quin said. "He looks kind of like . . ."

"He looks *exactly* like him — our Shadow!" I said. "Quin, it's him. The shape of the head, the pointy ears, those peculiar eyes, the dark fur. He's the spitting image of the dog at the cabin. You probably got even a better look at him than I did — don't you think it's him?"

"It could be," Quin said. "Any dog could have that coloring, but you're right about the shape of the face and the ears. And the eyes."

"Is there anything on the back?" I asked excitedly. "Turn it over!"

Quin turned the picture over.

"It says something, but it's really faded," she said. "Hang on."

She got off the bed and carried the picture over to a light.

She held the photo directly under the lamp and squinted. Then her face changed to confusion.

"What?" she murmured.

"Can you read it?" I asked eagerly. "Is there a name?"

Quin nodded.

"What is it?" I pressed, barely able to contain myself. "Quin! What's the name?"

She looked up at me with a perplexed expression.

"Balto. This is a picture of Balto."

DODIE

A late blizzard came that May, roaring over us with no warning one morning. Silla had gone for a walk with Caspian, though she wasn't supposed to. She told me she had dreamed of gold again, and she meant to follow the old creek into the woods up to a spot where the water pooled. Silla always said she was sure there was one more nugget of gold in that pool, and that she meant to keep looking until she found it. Sometimes I went with her, and though I didn't like her to go alone, I never worried about her as long as Caspian was there. I knew he'd protect her with every ounce of strength he had, and he was a powerful dog.

By the afternoon there was more than a foot of snow on the ground, and Silla had not come back. In my heart, I had not begun to worry. Silla knew as well as anyone that the best thing to do was hunker down and take shelter until the snow stopped. There was little by the way of shelter out by the creek, though. Silla would have to dig an ice cave in the snow and sit tight. My father was almost out of his mind with worry, so I told him what I knew, that Silla was with Caspian at the wide pool in Dorothy Creek, and that Caspian would keep her safe — and when the snow let up, he would lead her home. I was so sure Daddy would feel better knowing that.

But he didn't. He went crazy, shouting at me, his face this terrible, angry red, yelling that the woods were dangerous, that Caspian was dangerous, and that it was my fault for letting Silla go, and his for letting Caspian anywhere near her. There was nothing I could do to convince him that it would be all right. He simply would not listen to me. But even Daddy knew he could not go out looking for a lost child in the middle of a blizzard. We would have to wait for the snow to stop.

It did not stop. The wind blew and the snow came down for three days and three nights. On the fourth morning, I woke up with a sick certainty in my heart. Too much time had passed. Silla had not been strong to begin with, and her lungs were bad. No matter where she might have taken shelter, Silla would not survive the storm this long.

The morning the storm finally broke, my father was downstairs throwing things in a pack, to rush out and search for Silla. In my heart, I knew he would not find her. The little buzz I always felt, the bright bauble of Silla's presence in my own spirit, was gone. But I did not want my father to go out searching alone, and I was determined to go with him whether he liked it or not. I had to run to keep up with him as he got onto the path into the woods, following the direction of the creek. The creek I was named for.

We hadn't been following the creek for more than a half mile when Caspian came bolting toward us. His eyes were wild again, like they'd been that morning the wolf went after the pups. His muzzle, mouth, and teeth were covered in blood, and with each step he left a crimson paw print in the snow. Why would Daddy have thought that blood was Silla's? How could he have jumped to a conclusion so wrong?

But he did. Every doubt he'd ever had about Caspian, all the worries that the dog had a savage nature, might again turn on humans, returned. Before I could stop him he had raised his shotgun and was pointing the barrel at Caspian's great chest. And Caspian simply stood there.

9

Quin was just as obsessed with getting to the bottom of the dog ghost story as I was. Neither of us had been able to get Shadow off her mind. Clay, Joe, and my dad had talked for several hours after dinner, and my father had been more than willing to say yes when Quin asked if I could sleep over. Jack would have been outraged to be left out, except that he had fallen asleep in front of the wood-burning stove. He never woke up when my father carried him to the car.

Long past midnight, Quin and I sat in front of her laptop, searching for information about Balto. We fell asleep with the laptop still lying open on the bed and kept sleeping until almost noon the next day.

"Okay, so let's go through this again," Quin said, pulling the blanket more tightly around her. I flipped my pillow over, fluffed it up a bit, and laid my head back down.

"Right, so Balto leads his team into Nome with the medicine in February of 1925, and all the sick people are saved," I said. "There's a big to-do about it — all the newspapers have stories about him. The musher, Gunnar Kaasen, ends up taking Balto and the whole team on a cross-country lecture tour of America so people can hear the story and see the dogs."

"Then somehow all the dogs end up being left in California," Quin continued. "It's too hot there and the dogs get sick. Then a bunch of kids in Ohio donate pennies and raise enough money to buy them."

I pulled more covers onto me, and Quin yanked them back.

"Sorry," I said. "So the dogs retire in comfort at the Cleveland zoo, and eventually — what, six or seven years later? — Balto dies of old age."

"Yep," Quin said. "Just doesn't make any sense. Why would he be haunting some old cabin up by Dorothy Creek when he died thousands of miles away, and hadn't even been in Alaska for, like, ten years?"

"I don't know," I said. "Okay, what if something happened in that cabin before the epidemic in Nome? Do we know who owned Balto, where he was from?"

Quin pulled the laptop toward her.

"Google 'who owned Balto,'" I suggested.

"I just did, genius," Quin said. "This is interesting. Balto was actually owned by Leonhard Seppala."

"The guy from the old picture holding the big white dog?" I said, sitting up and leaning toward her to get a better look at the screen.

"Yep," she said. "He seems to have been a big deal back then. Apparently a lot of great working dogs came from the Seppala kennels. Okay, it also says Seppala himself was one of the mushers that helped run the medicine to Nome, but he didn't take Balto because he thought he was too young and inexperienced. His favorite dog was Togo and he took him as the team leader. He left Balto behind, and somehow Gunnar Kaasen ended up taking him with his team."

She set down the laptop and looked at me. "If Balto was a young dog being raised and trained in Seppala's kennel, I can't see any way he would have ended up out by Dorothy Creek in some miner's cabin, ever."

I sighed. Quin was right. It didn't make any sense. But I badly wanted to know more about the ghost, and the photo was our only lead.

"I need to see the picture again," I said.

"It's on my desk," Quin told me.

106

I got out of bed. The floor was freezing — the whole house felt cold. I grabbed the picture as quickly as I could while still being careful, and hurried back to the warm bed.

There was a small skylight in the sloped ceiling just above the bed, and daylight streamed in. I looked at the picture carefully.

"Quin, look at the face. The shape of it, the way the mouth curls up a tiny bit at the edges like he's smiling. And those pale eyes. I could still swear it's Shadow."

"Gimme," Quin said, holding out her hand.

I handed over the picture.

"It could be," she said. "Then again, how many malamutes and huskies with all dark fur were there in Alaska in 1925? Hundreds, maybe? This looks a lot like him, but in reality, what are the odds? We see a ghost dog out in the wilderness and it turns out to be the most famous sled dog in Alaskan history? I mean, we don't even know what time period our dog is from. He could have been alive in Balto's time, or it could have been just twenty years ago."

I sighed again.

"I just wish we could get a better look at Balto," I said. "A different view instead of just his face."

Quin smacked her forehead.

"Stupidy-dumb! Balto's famous — we can just Google Image him!"

She typed something and hit enter. A moment later, she sighed, and turned the laptop toward me so I could see the screen.

"Well, I found a picture of Balto standing. Look at his chest."

I did.

"He has a big patch of white fur," I said.

"Yep. Shadow is black from head to tail. I hate to say it, but it looks like we've been barking up the wrong tree."

I groaned, half from disappointment and half from Quin's terrible pun.

"Darn it. All right, then. So we're back to square one."

"I don't think we even have a square one," Quin said. "It's not like we have a picture of Shadow to work from."

I sat up and stared at Quin.

"That's it!" I said. "My camera! We could get a picture of him. The whole reason my father is here is to talk to the people who were around sixty years ago when everyone had teams — the people who knew everyone's dogs. People like that Dorothy Shaktoolik. People like Clay! Somebody might recognize him."

"Let me get this straight," Quin said, pulling the covers up to her chin. "You're suggesting we hike back out to the cabin, bring your camera, and hang around in the brush waiting for a dog ghost to come back so we can snap a picture of him?"

"Well . . . yeah," I said.

A grin slowly crept across Quin's face.

"Tee, my friend," she said. "Now you're talking."

A quick telephone call home to my father, and we had permission for Quin to come spend the night with me. Joe offered to drive us to our cabin, but not until later in the afternoon.

"I was sort of hoping we'd be able to hike back to the cabin today," I said to Quin, disappointed, watching her create two lopsided ham sandwiches as we stood at the kitchen counter. "But I guess we'll have to save it for tomorrow morning."

"It's already late — we slept half the day. Going tomorrow is better anyway," Quin said, taking the top off her sandwich to plop an additional spoonful of mayonnaise on it. "Do you want more mayo?"

"There's never enough mayo," I said. Quin pulled the top piece of bread off my sandwich too, and added a huge dollop.

"There. Made to order. Okay — so, while we eat, we need to think about what we bring in our packs. We're going to want to dress really warmly. It's one thing to be out in this weather hiking. If we end up having to stand around waiting for the dog to show up, we're going to get really cold really fast. Plus, this is Alaska — we need to check the weather report right up until the minute we leave. They've been talking about snow coming this week, and believe me, you have *never* seen snow until you've seen it here. April is not too late for a storm."

"I'm ridiculously excited about this," I said, taking the plate with my lunch and sitting across the table from Quin. "It's so nice to have something to look forward to, for a change. I have this feeling we're going to do it. We're going to get a picture of Shadow. I just wish we didn't have to wait until tomorrow morning!"

"Well, we do," she said firmly. "Dad can't even take us to your place for another two hours. But hey, I know what we can do in the meantime — we can go see Clay and ask what he knows about the history of Dorothy Creek. He lives just two houses down."

"Really? You don't think he'd mind?" I loved the idea of seeing Clay again.

"Are you kidding? Clay lives for company," Quin said. "I think he's kind of lonely. And he always has the best cake."

"Cake? Lead the way," I said.

We finished our sandwiches quickly, gulping down milk as we stood in the warmth of the wood-burning stove. Quin ducked into her father's office to let him know where we were going, then we pulled on our fleeces and hats and went outside. The sky was a brilliant, cloudless blue and the sun shone warmly, making the air feel a little warmer than it actually was.

"This way," Quin said, pointing to her left.

Clay's was exactly two houses down. It looked even smaller than Quin's house — no second floor at all. But it was freshly painted a deep blue, and it looked well cared for.

Quin knocked on the door, then opened it slightly.

"Clay?" she called. "It's Quin and Tee."

I heard the sound of footsteps, and suddenly the door swung all the way open. Clay looked like he'd known somebody was going to stop by, because he was dressed in a spiffy deep blue flannel shirt and neat jeans, his snow white hair combed carefully into place.

"Well looky here — two rays of sunshine, right on my doorstep! Darn it, but I'm a lucky guy. Come on in!"

I looked around curiously as we walked inside. I was struck by how incredibly neat it was, and by the absence of clutter. Like Quin's home, most of the ground floor was a combined kitchen and living room area dominated by a wood-burning stove. A kettle had been set to boil on a burner on top of the stove. The cabin was furnished with a couch, a solid dining table with four chairs, and a large chest beneath a window. There was a closed door I presumed led to a bedroom and bathroom. With Clay standing in the middle of the room smiling broadly at us, it seemed like the most cheerful and welcoming place on earth.

"You know, I was just this morning wondering what to do with this big old slab of lemon cake I got sitting here," Clay said. "Would you two help a fella out by taking some of it off my hands?"

"We'd love some," Quin said. "I'll get the tea ready."

Quin opened a cabinet and pulled out a teapot and a tin of dry tea while Clay unwrapped the wax paper from the cake. From the way she knew where everything was in the kitchen, I could tell Quin was a frequent guest here.

A few minutes later we were sitting near the wood-burning stove, each of us with a mug of spiced tea and a massive slab of lemon cake.

"Mmm," Quin said, her mouth full. "Best this month, Clay."

"You may be right," he said. "Come back tonight and we'll have the rest for dinner."

"I wish," Quin said. "But I'm going to sleep over at Tee's tonight. We've got a big hike planned for tomorrow. Up by Dorothy Creek."

Clay looked at me, then back at Quin.

"You'll need to keep an eye on the forecast," he said. "There'll be some snow coming this week. Could be a few days off, or it could come sooner."

"We will, I promise," Quin said. "Clay, whose land is that up there?"

"That'd be the Shaktooliks', I guess," Clay said, dunking a piece of cake into his tea and popping it into his mouth. "Don't know why they don't just sell some of it off. Most of those grandkids are in Anchorage or Juneau now, and Marilyn lives here in town. And Pete and Clyde got no use for it. Maybe Doe just doesn't want anyone else to have it."

"We found an old falling-down cabin up there the last time we hiked," Quin said.

"Yeah?" Clay asked.

"We thought it might be an old miners' cabin," I added.

"Well, that could be," Clay said. "Plenty of prospectors went panning the creek and thereabouts back in the day. Or could have been someone who worked for the Shaktooliks — they had a big place up there they built before the war."

"You mean . . . Iraq?" I asked.

Clay smiled. "Vietnam," he clarified.

"I didn't know there was ever a house out there," Quin said.

"Well, the weather probably took most of it back by now," Clay said.

"Why would someone just abandon their house?" Quin pressed. Clay put his mug down and looked out the window a moment, his eyes distant with memory.

"They just couldn't bear the memories, I guess. Touched by tragedy, the Shaktooliks were. They had a string of bad luck. Lost a son in Vietnam. And then that little girl died, or maybe it happened the other way around. Anyway, I guess that was about all they could take."

"What little girl?" I asked, with a strange feeling of foreboding.

Clay kept looking out the window. Then he shook his head.

"That was a long time ago," he said. "It was the youngest child. Something happened to her. In those days there were so many things that could carry a child off — fever, accident, a long winter with too much snow and not enough food. I don't remember now exactly what it was. Only thing that sticks out in my mind is the Shaktooliks packed up and left their place after she passed."

"That's so sad," I said, thinking of a home abandoned to the woods because a family was grieving for a lost child.

"It sure is," he replied, his eyes grave.

His face grew somber for a moment, and I wondered what his story was. Where was his family? Did he have children? Why did he now live alone?

"Clay, do you believe in ghosts?" Quin asked suddenly.

"I'm surprised a girl as smart as you would even think to ask such a fool question," he replied.

I looked at him curiously. He was staring into his mug, shaking his head.

"I've lived in Nome most all my life, seen things you'd never believe. Seen people come and go, wars come and go. Storms come and go. Things in the snow, things in the woods. Never got much book learning, but I've got more life learning than most."

He put his mug down, and looked from me to Quin.

"Of course I believe. I know what's real, and what's real is what I can see with these two eyes in my head," he said. "That's how come I believe in ghosts."

"Then you've seen one?" I asked.

"Sure I have," Clay said. "Seen way more than one. If you know where to look, there's ghosts *everywhere*."

10

"And Clay gave us this unbelievable cake, Dad — it was so good I almost died. He's really nice, and Quin says he's lived there all by himself for as long as anyone seems to remember. Do you really think you might be able to interview him in the book?"

"Oh, definitely," my father said. "He knows a lot about the Iditarod and about dogs, even ones from way back when, who everybody else has forgotten about. And boy, can he tell a story."

The mention of dogs everybody had forgotten about reminded me of Shadow, who was the real reason I was standing in my dad's office late at night, while Quin curled up patiently in a camp bed in my room.

"I actually wanted to ask you if it would be okay if Quin and I took a hike just by ourselves tomorrow," I said. "Without Jack," I added. "We'd be taking the same trail I've been exploring, but we want to go a bit farther, and you know how Jack can get. We just really, really want to go by ourselves."

My father took his glasses off, and leaned back in the ancient desk chair he had padded with a variety of pillows. His eyes looked tired, as they always did when he read and took notes all day.

"You really like Quin, don't you?" he asked me.

"I do, Dad. She's amazing!"

"I like Joe, too," he said. "They're good people."

"So would it be okay for tomorrow morning? You're going to be here and everything, so Jack won't be alone? For our hike, I mean?"

"Oh. Sure. You guys plan on that. You'll have a great time."

I gave him a quick hug, and he hugged me back, still clutching a paper in his right hand that made a crinkling sound.

"Thanks!" I called, dancing back to my room.

"He said yes!" I told Quin.

Lazily ensconced in the camp bed under numerous blankets with the *Zodiac Guide* clutched in one hand, Quin gave me a happy thumbs-up.

Quin and I were still sleeping the next morning, Henry snoring at my feet, when I heard my dad moving around.

I checked the clock — it was just before eight. Quin showed no signs of stirring. I got out of bed quietly, grabbing my heavy shearling slippers and pulling a sweatshirt on before wrapping my robe over it.

"You made coffee already?" I asked, walking into the kitchen.

"Hey, you're up," Dad said, pouring the steaming coffee into a thermos. "I was just going to write you a note. I need to run into town to pick up a box from the historical society. They're letting me borrow the old newspapers from the twenties. I cannot wait to start going through them!"

"Wait, you're going into Nome now?" I asked.

"Yeah, but I won't be that long. Should be back by two or three."

I felt a flash of frustration rising in my throat. I took a deep breath.

"Quin and I are supposed to be going on a hike this morning, remember? I talked about it with you last night, to make sure someone would be home with Jack. You said we could go."

My father looked stricken.

"Oh geez, you're right — I completely forgot about that."

It was less than twelve hours ago — how could he have forgotten about it already?

"No, I mean, it's okay," I said. "You have a lot of things to remember right now. But, you know, we'd still really like to do that. Go on the hike."

"I'll make it back as quick as I can," he said. "But I want to get those papers today. The weather report says we may get some snow overnight, and Joe told me that could mean anything from a dusting to a flat-out blizzard, in which case none of us will be going anywhere tomorrow. So I've got to make sure I've got that box before the weather hits."

I tried to keep the disappointment off my face, reminding myself that the whole reason we were in Alaska was for my father's work.

"Okay," I said.

"You're an angel, Sweet Tee," he said. "And who knows, maybe it will take less time than I think and you guys can go when I get back."

I nodded without saying anything, because suddenly I was afraid I might start to cry. I walked back into my room, shutting the door quietly. Henry lifted his head sleepily and stared at me. I stood there listening as my father muttered to himself, then came down the hall and went out the door.

When I heard the sound of the car engine starting, a fat tear rolled down my cheek. It was quickly followed by another. I knelt next to the foot of the bed and pressed my face against Henry's soft neck.

"What's going on?" Quin asked. "Hey, are you crying? What happened?"

I rubbed the tears from my face and shook my head.

"Nothing happened, it's just . . . my dad just left. He's going into Nome for the morning."

Quin sat up.

"Are you kidding me?" she asked.

"He said he forgot. He has to get some research material now, in case the snow comes today."

"But that's not fair," Quin said.

"I don't know," I said. "I mean, it's his research. It's why we came to Alaska in the first place."

"No," Quin said. "It's why *he* came to Alaska. But he brought two other people along with him. What about you?"

I stared at her.

"What do you mean?" I asked.

Quin sighed and said gently, "No offense, but from the few times I've been here, it seems like you do a lot of helping out."

"Not any more than other people," I said. "Okay, more than some. But we're only here for two weeks, and this time is really important to my dad."

"I know that," Quin said. "But he specifically said we could go out to that cabin. Then this morning he's all like 'Whoops, I forgot'? Did he even say he was sorry?"

I stared at Quin. Part of me wanted to lash out at her, because I hated hearing anything negative about my father. When my mother was off on one of her business trips, he depended on me. He always said so, and it made me feel proud.

But I didn't feel proud now. I felt angry.

"No," I muttered, sitting back on the floor, as Henry watched me with mournful eyes. "He didn't say he was sorry. And he certainly didn't offer to change his plans."

"That's what I mean," Quin told me. "He shouldn't act like it's no big deal. You do more than your fair share of chores around the house. It's not okay that you don't get to be a kid every once in a while."

"You know what? You're right," I said, getting to my feet.

"Okay, well, that's all I'm saying," Quin said.

I stood in the middle of the room, allowing Quin's words to really sink in. She had just verbalized in one easy sentence what had been smoldering in the pit of my stomach for a long time. When did I ever ask for anything for myself? My mother's trips were getting longer and longer, and more stuff was falling to me. How, the one time I asked for something for me, could my father just forget about it like it meant nothing?

"Aren't you freezing?" she asked me. "Might as well just come back to bed, since we don't have a hike to pack for now."

"No," I said. "I'm not freezing."

"Okay then, stand there and let your lips turn blue."

All I had asked for was a few hours to take a hike.

And I wanted that hike.

"What are you just standing there for? You look like you're having an out-of-body experience or something."

"Get up," I said. "We've got to pack for the hike."

Quin sat back up in bed and stared at me, confused.

"But . . . I don't understand. You just said your dad wasn't coming back until this afternoon."

I nodded.

"I did. But you know what? You are absolutely right about this not being okay. Do you know why my father didn't apologize? Because he didn't think I cared. Which is *my* fault. For the past year, since my mom's career has gotten crazy busy, I have never ever *once* complained. I've never asked for anything for myself, and I've always acted like there was nothing in the world I wanted to be doing but babysitting Jack or making meat loaf. For once, I want to hang out with my friend and not be on duty the whole time!"

I started breathing in and out quickly, the way a person does when they're about to cry.

"Okay. It's okay," Quin said. "Look, it's good that you're realizing that. You just need to tell your dad the same thing."

"But there's no point in talking to him, because he obviously doesn't listen to me," I said, my voice sounding unusually high. "He certainly wasn't listening last night when I jumped up and down like an idiot thanking him for giving me permission to go on one measly walk. We're only here for maybe one more week. I have to find Shadow, get a picture of him — find out what he needs. I have to help him! For all I know there's never going to be a day my dad actually agrees to hang out here. So we *are* going on that hike, and we're going now. Jack is just sleeping. There's no flippin' way I'm sitting around here listening to him breathe when we could be out on the trail."

Quin looked taken aback.

"But what if he . . . I mean, you know your brother better than I do, obviously," Quin said. "But . . . do you really feel okay about leaving him by himself after he ended up waking up and finding us gone the last time?"

"If he wakes up, he wakes up," I snapped. "He doesn't need a security guard standing over him twenty-four hours a day. I am going to that cabin. If you want to stay here and baby Jack, then do it."

My voice had gotten progressively louder. I hated the way I sounded — I hated the way I felt.

"No, I'm coming with you," Quin said, getting quickly out of bed. "But at least leave him a note, okay?"

"Fine," I said, grabbing my pack. "Whatever. Just hurry up."

Ten minutes later we had two full packs, stuffed with extra layers of clothes, protein bars, water, a compass, a topographical map, and the camera. I scrawled a note to Jack saying we were out walking with Henry and not to worry.

"I feel like we're forgetting something," Quin said, staring at her pack.

"We're fine. Quin, we're only going to be gone a couple of hours. We've got plenty — let's move!"

Henry, who had been watching our packing curiously, stood up expectantly as I zipped up my fleece. I knelt down, wrapped my arms around his neck, and kissed his soft ears.

"Good boy, buddy," I murmured. "You ready to help us go find Shadow?"

Henry's eyes were bright with happiness and his tail was going a mile a minute as I got his leash down and attached it through the ring on his collar. Quin waited for me to finish. My hand was on the latch when the door to Jack's room opened and he came into the hallway.

"Uh-oh," muttered Quin.

"Go back to sleep, Jack," I told my brother.

Jack stood where he was, his hair standing up on his head and his little arms folded across his chest. Something about his expression made me suspect he'd heard some, or maybe all, of what I'd said to Quin earlier.

"What's happening?" he asked. "Why are you mad?"

"Quin and I are going on a hike, that's all," I said. "Just go back to sleep, and we'll be back before you know it."

"Are you going to see the dog ghost?" Jack asked.

"No," I lied.

"Yes you are," he insisted. "I heard you talking. I want to go too."

"No," I snapped.

"But —"

"Jack, I said NO!"

Jack flinched, and his eyes filled with tears. I sighed, put my pack down, and walked over to him.

"Sorry," I said. "We're just in kind of a hurry. You can go with us next time."

"But why can't —"

"Next time," I repeated, my voice rising again. I put my hand on his back, and nudged him toward his room. "Just go back to bed. Seriously. I cannot deal with this right now."

Jack allowed me to guide him back to his room, but he turned and looked at me, hurt and confused.

"Why are you mad at me?" he asked.

I gave his shoulder a little squeeze.

"I'm not mad at you," I said. "Maybe I'm a little mad at Alaska, or something. We'll talk when I get back, okay? Okay?"

His lower lip trembled a little.

"Can Henry stay with me?" he asked.

"He's coming with us," I said, as Jack's face fell even further. "He needs the exercise, Jack. You know that. Look, just go back to bed and stay there — we'll be home before you know it, and we'll do something fun. Your new Nintendo game — anything you want. Okay?"

I pretended not to notice that Jack's face said he was really not okay about any of this. I gave him a gentle nudge, and he obediently trotted into his room, turning to give me a confused look as I shut his door and ignored the huge tide of guilt rising in me.

"Let's go," I said to Quin.

She opened her mouth to ask a question, but I pushed past her and opened the front door, letting Henry shoot out first. I hid the relief I felt as she followed me outside without questioning me further. I was absolutely determined to go, no matter what, even if Quin decided to stay behind with Jack. In spite of what I'd said, I definitely didn't want to go looking for Shadow by myself.

We walked quickly and in silence for about ten minutes, Henry energetically taking the lead. I could feel Quin giving me the occasional curious look. I knew she was surprised at my sudden act of rebellion. I was surprised by it too. I didn't like the feelings of resentment that had sprung up in my heart. I'd been pushing them down for so many months, ignoring everything, waiting for them to go away. But now I could not ignore them — I could not ignore the chorus that kept running through my head.

What about me? What about me?

"Tee!" Quin said. "Can we slow it down just a little?"

I realized that the angrier I got, the faster I'd been walking. My heart was pounding and I was out of breath.

"Sorry," I said, slowing down.

"Let's just keep it to a slow sprint," she said. "We're making good time."

I adjusted my pack slightly, and shivered when the sun went behind a cloud. The temperature was well below freezing, and without the sun it felt even colder.

"Oh no," Quin exclaimed. "I just remembered what we forgot."

"Oh well," I said.

"Seriously. We forgot to check the weather report," she said. "That was really important. Maybe we should —"

"We're practically there," I said. "It's sunny out. It's not going to snow in the next hour."

"It's actually not sunny anymore," Quin said. "And no offense, but I've lived in Nome for three years. I think I know more about the weather here than you do."

"Fine," I said, coming to a sudden stop, causing Henry to spin back around as his leash went taut. "Go back, then. Listen to the stupid weather forecast. I don't care. I'm going to find Shadow."

Quin grabbed my arm.

"Will you just stop it?" she cried.

"Stop what?"

"Every time I ask a question, you get all — 'fine, I'll go myself!' I'm on your side. I'm with you. I'm not going to flounce back to the cabin or something. Don't bite my head off just because I'm pointing out that we forgot to do something important."

I started to say I wasn't biting anyone's head off, but my voice didn't come out right. I felt tears coming into my eyes. Quin squeezed my elbow again.

"I'm on your side," she repeated. "Don't worry about Jack — he'll be fine, and we'll make it up to him this afternoon, just like you said."

As soon as the words were out of Quin's mouth, I realized this it wasn't only anger at my father that was making me feel so terrible. It was guilt, for leaving Jack by himself. I wondered how Quin could know something about me before I even knew it myself.

"I know you're on my side," I said, looking at her. "I know you're my friend. I'm yours too."

Quin's face, already flushed from the cold, reddened a little more. She smiled at me.

"Okay, then. Let's go," she said. "That's the place where the trail branches off, right there, isn't it?"

"Oh yeah," I said. "Wow, we did make good time. Do you remember exactly where the cabin is from here?"

"Yep," Quin said, pointing, then heading toward a clump of bushes and low trees. "Through here."

I was glad Quin remembered, because all the clumps out here looked exactly the same to me. I pushed through the branches, keeping Henry's leash tight, getting caught up a couple of times when my pack snagged on something. It was a little easier this time since we'd blazed a path of sorts when we forced our way through the last time. Quin seemed to wiggle right through like an eel.

"Quin, wait," I called. I knew she was just ahead of me, but having her out of my sight made me feel panicked. There was just one place where the bushes were especially thick and I was having trouble getting through with Henry. I picked him up in my arms, then put my head down and shoved my way forward, hoping I wasn't ripping my pack or my fleece in the process. Moments later I was free, standing in the clearing, just behind Quin. There was the cabin, looking gloomier and more decrepit than I remembered it. With the sun still behind clouds, everything looked eerily dark. I gently put Henry back on the ground. He took one look at the cabin and tried to back through the bushes the way we came. I pulled him to my side.

"I don't think Shadow's here," Quin said.

"Are you sure?" I asked.

"No," she said. "But I don't feel what I felt last time."

Quin walked to the door of the cabin, then disappeared inside. Remembering the uncomfortable damp and ruined feeling of the remains of the cabin's interior, I decided to stay where I was. A moment later, Quin came back out.

"I really don't think he's here," she said again. "I don't see anything, don't feel anything."

"So we wait?" I asked.

It had seemed like such a good idea yesterday. Now I wasn't so sure. I wasn't feeling any less guilty about leaving Jack behind, and my toes were already numb with the cold. But we'd come all this way.

"We could sit over there," Quin said, pointing. "See that rock? It's close enough to those little trees that we won't be right out in the open."

"Okay," I agreed.

We walked over to the rock, took off our packs, and sat down together, our shoulders touching. I looped Henry's leash around my foot and cinched it, but he'd be okay. As long as I was sitting, he'd stay sitting too, or he'd lie down and go to sleep. I unzipped my pack and pulled out the camera, checking the battery and making sure it was all set to go. Then we sat in silence for what seemed like an eternity, though it was likely not more than ten or fifteen minutes. My feet and fingers ached with cold, and my face felt numb. I was hungry, but the thought of taking off my gloves to open the protein bars was unbearable. The light kept fading. More than ever I wanted to see Shadow again. I wanted to photograph him, but even more, I wanted him to see me. I wanted to connect with him like Quin did, so that he'd know people cared what happened to him. What *had* happened to him.

But I knew I couldn't stand the cold much longer.

I was about to say something to Quin when I heard a sound. She turned toward me, her eyebrows raised. She had heard it too. Henry's head came up too, his ears pricked, his nose twitching, and his tail slightly wagging. We listened intently, and the sound came again, and another.

Something was moving through the bushes. Coming toward us.

Another twig snapped. I fumbled for my camera, then took off my gloves so I could work it better. I trained the lens toward the bushes where the noise was coming from.

Henry did not move at all, just kept his eyes on the bush, his tail still wagging a little. There was more rustling, then the branches of the bush itself were parting. I tried to steady my shaking hands as I looked through the viewfinder and pressed the button. The image froze on the view screen, and I'd captured the moment perfectly, a face emerging from the bushes. But it wasn't a dog.

It was the face of my brother, Jack.

DODIE

My screams not to shoot fell on deaf ears. Neither Daddy nor Caspian seemed to hear them. So I lunged forward, pushing my father as hard as I could. He lost his balance, and the shot he fired off went over Caspian's head.

Even then, Caspian remained standing there, so rigidly, with such urgency, needing us to know something.

But Daddy didn't mean to let Caspian live another moment. Like me, he knew in his heart that Silla was already gone. No child with weak lungs could survive three days and three nights in that storm with no food or water, not even with Caspian to protect her. Something in my father's mind had already snapped, and from the wild look in his eyes I knew he believed Caspian had killed Silla. Now he was going to kill Caspian.

I could not let that happen. I took hold of the barrel of the shotgun with both fists, angling it hard down toward the ground, and I shouted at Caspian to run. He took a single step forward and his eyes locked with mine. I felt his sorrow over the shock of the second gunshot. While I was still struggling with my father, Caspian turned and ran back the way he'd come. By the time my father was able to push me into the snow and raise the shotgun once more, Caspian was gone. No one would ever see him again.

They never found Silla. When the snow finally melted and summer came, maybe twenty-five people combed the woods looking for her, searched every inch of ground surrounding the pool in Dorothy Creek. But not a trace of her turned up. My father told everyone that Caspian had killed her, that he was a dangerous dog and anyone seeing him should shoot him on sight. There was no reasoning with Daddy. I believe by this time his mind was dangerously unstable. It took only one more thing to break it entirely.

Three weeks after Silla disappeared, a telegraph arrived informing us that Jim had been killed in Vietnam. My mother took to her bed, and my father was simply ruined. He began selling off the dogs, letting the buildings fall into disrepair. My youngest brother's tour had not yet begun and Clyde had received his assignment from the army to serve stateside. Between the two of them, my brothers finally convinced my parents to move into town.

I didn't want to leave this place where I had lived all my life — where Silla and I had played with countless puppies, where there was space and quiet enough to read the wind — where I could watch the northern lights dance in the sky. Where somewhere, my beloved Silla had died and Caspian as good as gone. I was almost eighteen now, old enough to live on my own. I wanted to move my belongings to Vernon's old place, which stood empty. My father agreed, for he did not want me in town with him. Daddy blamed me for Silla's death — blamed me for letting her go into the woods with Caspian. I know he did, because he told me so. You killed her, he said. You and that dog. And for my part, I was still looking for Caspian every day, hoping to find him before some friend of my father's with a shotgun did.

So I moved into Vernon's little cottage. Each day, though it was scarcely noticeable, the woods and brush grew a little closer toward my home. I went out every day, looking for Caspian. Calling for him. For the first few months I thought I caught sight of him every now and then, a long way off. I'd find a paw print, or a tuft of his fur on the ground. Many nights I felt he was watching me in the cottage. I'd open the door and call his name, but he wouldn't come forward from the shadows. Still, I knew he was out there, watching over me. He was silent but the force of his presence was unmistakable, as real and miraculous as the northern lights themselves.

I never saw Caspian again. After a year or so, I stopped believing I was catching glimpses of him. That second year, I no longer sensed him outside at night. I was truly alone. I suppose I could have packed up and moved into town then, found a little place. But I'd been out on my own so long, I wasn't sure I knew how to live among people anymore. At least here, even as the woods crept steadily toward my front door, I had Caspian and Silla. I was as close to either of them as I was ever going to get, ever again.

11

"I told you to stay home!" I shouted, as Henry got to his feet and wagged his tail wildly in welcome. Of course — he was a scent hound. He'd known all along it was Jack coming through the brush.

"You can't tell me what to do!" Jack yelled back. "Only Dad and Mom can!"

My mouth dropped open. All the guilt I had been feeling about leaving him behind instantly evaporated.

"Are you serious? Who watches you all day? Who helps you with your homework? Who makes sure you brush your teeth? Who plays your stupid DS games with you? I do! Me! I do all of it by myself, so guess what — I *do* get to tell you what to do!"

"My games aren't stupid!" Jack shot back.

"You are *not* supposed to be here," I cried. "This is the

one thing I wanted to do alone with my friend, and you're ruining it!"

"Both of you cut it out," Quin said sharply. "Shadow is never going to come back while you guys are standing here hollering at each other."

"Quin's right," I said. "Jack, go home."

"No," he said, folding his arms and staring at me defiantly. "You can't make me."

It was true. Short of carrying him back, I couldn't force Jack to go anywhere.

"Fine," I said. "Do whatever you want. I don't care. As far as I'm concerned, you're not here, Jack. As far as I'm concerned, you do not exist."

Jack flinched as if he'd been hit, and I instantly regretted my words. But before I could take it back, Quin grabbed my arm.

"Tee — it's snowing."

Jack and I looked up at the same time. Sure enough, fat snowflakes were falling from the sky.

"Snow!" Jack exclaimed. "Awesome!"

"Not awesome," Quin said firmly. "We need to head home right now."

"It's just a couple flakes," I said.

"Listen to me," Quin said, "because I'm being dead serious. We need to go *this instant*."

All of the determination I'd felt to find Shadow again suddenly left me. Between my father forgetting his promise, Jack showing up, and the reality of sitting in the woods in below-freezing temperatures, I just couldn't do it anymore.

"All right," I said. "Let's go, then."

"I don't want to go — I want to see the dog!" Jack argued.

Really, my little brother might be the most irritating person on the planet. What an idiot he was to follow us — he wasn't even wearing his stupid hat!

"Stay here, then, I don't care," I snapped. I shoved my camera in my pack, zipped it up, and slung it over one shoulder. Without waiting for Quin, I scooped Henry up in my arms and pushed back through the cluster of bushes. So many of the branches had now been broken off, I got through much faster and soon was on the other side. I set Henry down and we started up the hill, and after a moment I heard Quin's and Jack's voices, so I knew they were close behind me. I was working up to my angry quick pace again when I reached the top of the hill. What I saw brought me to a sudden stop.

In the direction of home, the sky was a deep, greenish black. What moments ago had been just a few flakes was now a swirling cloud, as if we were in a giant snow globe. My face was hit with a gust of wind so strong it forced me off balance several steps. Henry's ears blew straight back, like he was at a fashion shoot standing in front of one of those enormous fan things. Quin was suddenly at my elbow. When I turned to look at her, I could see her expression was grim.

"Is this bad?" I asked her.

"It's not good," she said.

"That's so cool," Jack exclaimed, pointing at the sky.

"So we'll walk really fast," I suggested.

Quin shook her head.

"We can't take the chance. It's a half hour back to your place, minimum. That storm is coming fast."

It didn't look like it was coming all that fast to me. But I wasn't going to argue with Quin. If she was worried, that was all I needed to know.

"What should we do?"

"We need to take shelter," she said. "And there's no place nearby except for that old cabin."

"But half the roof is gone," I said. "It's not exactly shelter."

"It's better than sitting out in the open," Quin said.

142

We were hit with another gust of wind, but this time it did not fall away. The snow was falling more heavily now, and it blew sideways into our faces. For a moment, I couldn't distinguish between the trail and the sky — everything was painted over by a sheet of white.

Quin turned to double back through the brush, and I followed her, one hand firmly placed on Jack's back. Henry didn't need to be carried now — we'd forced a good path through. Jack grumbled loudly as I pushed him along, but that only made me push harder. His hair was already drenched.

"Whoa, we're going in there? Is that where the ghost dog is? Does the witch live there too? That place is wicked awesome!"

I kept my eyes on Quin's back, purposely not looking at the bleak cabin, and its doorway darkly standing open.

We'd just hang out there for a bit, long enough for the storm to pass over, and then we'd head home. At least, that's what I told myself as we walked into the dim interior.

"This corner still has roof over it, and our backs will be to the wind," Quin said, pointing.

"Yeah, okay," I agreed.

Quin pulled a nylon poncho from her pack and spread it out. It didn't seem to do much good — the old wooden floor was freezing.

"What happened to this place?" Jack asked, crossing to the pile of rubble where the roof had collapsed. "Did the people die? This is like the episode of *Galaxy Outlaws* when they got trapped in a cave and the land squids were hunting them only they didn't know it!"

"No land squids out here, kiddo," Quin assured him.

I could feel Jack looking at me, but I pretended I didn't notice.

"There's always something waiting to hunt you on *Galaxy Outlaws*. Even in the snowy places. Maybe it's the Abdominal Snowman!"

Quin laughed.

"That's *Abominable* Snowman, genius," she said. "And we don't have those in Alaska. We do have Sasquatch, though. He's the one that looks kind of like Chewbacca."

"Does he eat people?" Jack asked, racing to the front of the cabin to look out the ruined window.

"Only boys," Quin said. Then she laughed again as Jack turned around and gave her an alarmed look. "Look at your face! Relax, I'm kidding!"

"There's a little pile of rocks over there," Jack said. "Maybe somebody left them for a secret message."

I could feel Jack's eyes on me again. I pretended to be focusing on arranging my pack as a pillow. Jack dashed

144

over to the pile of rocks, reached in, and picked something up.

"Tee, look," Jack said. "Tee. Tee!"

I knew I was being childish and petty, but I couldn't seem to help myself. The more Jack tried to get my attention, the more I deliberately ignored him.

"Look at this — it's a golden button! It looks really old — is it from a treasure? Tee! Look at it!"

Something whizzed through the air and whacked my leg. Henry, curled up next to me, looked around wildly, hoping Jack had tossed a dog biscuit.

"Ow! Jack, that hurt! God, what did I do to deserve you?"

"I didn't mean for it to hit you," Jack muttered. I picked up the little gold thing Jack had thrown and almost whipped it back at him, but I stopped myself.

"You never mean it, what difference does it make?" I yelled. "It could have hit me in the face — but did you think of that? No! You always ruin everything! You do nothing but ruin my whole life!"

"Tee, geez, lighten up," Quin snapped. "Jack, come on. She didn't mean it."

Jack's face was scrunched up, his lips working uselessly to say something. I knew he was trying his hardest not to cry. Great — not content with feeling miserable myself, I'd now succeeded in making my little brother feel lousy too.

"Jack, I didn't mean that. *Jack.*"

Now he was the one ignoring me. I slipped the button into my pocket and got up, leaving Henry where he lay, and walked over to Jack. I reached out and grabbed his shoulder.

"I did not mean that."

"Nuh-uh. No backsies, no keepsies," he said grimly, but his posture had relaxed somewhat.

"Sorry, that doesn't work on me," I told him. "Listen, I was really mad at Dad for forgetting something he promised me, and I was taking it out on you. It is *not* your fault and you didn't do anything wrong. And I actually really like that DS game with the hedgehog."

"Sonic?" Jack asked, rubbing at his eyes with two balled-up fists.

"That one, yeah," I said.

"You're so terrible at it," he told me. "Quin, she can't even remember the difference between the A button and the B button."

I laughed.

"It's true," I admitted. "I need you to help me."

"Maybe I could help you when we get home," Jack offered.

"That'd be great," I said. Jack looked happier now, but I also noticed he was shivering. Streaks of frost covered his hair where the snow had melted on it. I put an arm around him to try to warm him up, but I was shivering too. Snow was blowing into the cabin, and the wind was rattling the loose boards of the wall behind us.

"Um, Quin . . . so when do you think that might be?" I asked. "You know, that we can head for home?"

Quin got up and walked a little stiffly to the door. Keeping one hand on the doorjamb, she leaned outside and looked around.

"Looks like it's turning into a real storm," she said. She dropped her voice even lower. "A blizzard, even."

"But it's April!" I said.

"And we're less than two hundred miles from Siberia. Your New York weather rules just don't apply here."

"No, I know that," I said. "It's just, it's getting even colder, and . . ."

I gestured toward Jack, who had sat down on the poncho, shaking with cold, one arm around Henry.

"I know," Quin said. "But ask anyone who lives here, and they'll tell you the same thing. If it's snowing hard, dig in and stay put. When it's blowing like this you can't tell the ground from the sky, and that's when you're likely to wander off in the wrong direction and get lost. And that is the last thing you want to happen."

Jack had started to sing, which is something he did sometimes at night when he woke up after a nightmare. I sat down and slid closer to him and put an arm around his shoulders.

For a while, Quin and I joined my little brother in singing, making our voices sound ridiculously high or flat or loud on purpose, to show Jack how totally cheerful we were, how funny the whole situation really was.

But we weren't cheerful, and it wasn't funny. We all sat close together, Quin and I on the outside, and Jack and Henry on the inside. Quin stopped singing first, then me. Finally Jack stopped too. The wind was now howling outside. I would have needed to shout to be heard. My hands, feet, and face were totally numb. Scarier than that was the deep sense of exhaustion I felt. I just wanted to go to sleep. And I didn't need Quin to tell me that if you fell asleep in the middle of a blizzard, you might well never wake up again.

Still, I was so tired. I felt as if hours had passed. How long could we do this? Even if my father made it back home and discovered us missing — even if he could figure out the direction we'd gone — there was no way he could come after us while the storm was going on. We were certainly stuck for the night. I had never been so cold in my life — how was I going to feel in eight hours when the sun was down and the temperatures dropped below zero?

Do not think about that, I told myself. I needed to just focus on getting through one minute. Then another. Then another. *Do it for Jack.*

Twice I caught myself nodding off and forced myself to wake up. Sleeping meant freezing to death. But it got to the point that it was hard to tell if I was sleeping or not. Everything took on a dreamlike quality. At one point Jack did seem to nod off, and when I woke him he was crying.

"Don't cry, Jackster," I said to him.

"I saw the witch," he whimpered. "She was outside in the snow. She was going to take us!"

"There's no witch, buddy," I told him.

"I'm hungry," he murmured.

There was nothing I could say to that. We were all hungry. Something about the bitter cold made an empty stomach feel much, much worse. It was going to be the longest night of our lives. It was just going to get harder and harder as each hour passed.

149

My face was so cold it was hard to form the words — I couldn't get my lips to move. Jack leaned his frozen-haired little head on my shoulder, and I felt tears spring into my eyes. This was my fault. If Quin and I hadn't snuck out, Jack would never have felt the need to follow us. He wouldn't be in a blizzard without a hat on. The tears on my eyelashes froze, and I had to rub my eyelids to keep them from sticking together.

Maybe it would be okay if I just closed my eyes for five seconds. I would be very disciplined about it — I would count, and make sure I opened my eyes before I got to the number six. This trick seemed to work a few times, but ultimately it just made me feel number and sleepier. My eyeballs themselves hurt, and I was having trouble seeing clearly.

When a shape seemed to darken the swirl of snow that the doorway framed, I thought I'd fallen asleep again and was dreaming. I closed my eyes tightly, with the reasoning that maybe I could wake myself up by opening them in the dream.

And it couldn't have worked, because when I did open my eyes, I saw a shape standing over me. A pair of pale blue, intelligent eyes was staring into mine. I knew those eyes. I knew that face. And what I saw meant I was probably dead. It was Shadow.

His ears were flattened, and his teeth bared in a snarl. He was low on his haunches, as if about to spring in attack. He did not mean well.

The dog ghost had come for us.

12

"Quin . . . do you . . ."

"I see him," Quin called out. She was just two feet away, but with gusts of wind rattling the shingles of the cabin, her voice seemed tiny and distant.

I sat up, trying to clear my head, and only then realized that we were covered by a blanket of snow. Henry was curled in a tiny circle, my arm around him on one side, and Jack's on the other.

"Shadow, go home," I said stupidly. "Go home."

But Shadow didn't listen. Instead, he took a step forward, and as I watched in horror, he bit my brother on the arm.

"Let him go, let him go!" I yelled.

"Stop it," Jack said, sounding confused.

I tried to get up now, to push myself between Shadow and Jack, but my legs were weak and my muscles aching. My knees seemed to be locked in place.

152

"Let him go!" I yelled again.

"Tee, stop it," Jack said. "He wants me to go with him. He wants us all to."

"Jack, no," I began, but Jack was already struggling to his feet. As soon as he got up, Shadow released his arm, and now I could see that he had only taken the sleeve of Jack's coat between his teeth.

"He wants us to go with him," Jack repeated.

I opened my mouth to say no again.

But really, what were our choices? We were not going to make it through the night here in the old cabin — not without help. If we followed Shadow outside we might freeze to death. But if we stayed here, we definitely would. Stay or go?

Quin answered my unasked question by struggling to her feet. She reached down and pulled on my arm. My legs felt like rubber, but I stood up, shakily.

"I think Jack's right," she said. "I think we should go with Shadow."

I would have given anything in the world at that moment to just say that I was too tired — to simply close my eyes and sink back into that blanket of snow. But ultimately Jack was going to do whatever I did. If I refused to follow Shadow, he would refuse too. And we would die here.

I forced myself to stay on my feet, though I felt as if my frozen soles were being stabbed by a thousand tiny needles.

"If we're going to go, then let's go now," I said.

I pulled on Henry's leash. My beagle opened one eye, then both. After a moment, he too reluctantly got to his feet.

Shadow turned and walked in silence to the door of the cabin, pausing once to glance at us before walking through. The four of us followed him outside.

The wind was terrible. It hurt my ears, my nose, my skin. The blowing snow stung like a slap. I saw a low, dark shape in front of me and realized Shadow had stopped. At that same moment, I saw there was something else there, another form hazily visible in the blowing snow. For a brief moment the wind died down and I caught a clearer look.

Several feet ahead of Shadow was the figure of a person, so wrapped up in layers I could not see if it was a man or a woman.

The figure was gesturing, and the meaning was crystal clear.

Follow me, quickly.

A strange, almost hysterical voice inside my head said, *It's the witch!*

The figure gestured again.

Jack, who I had by the arm, pulled forward.

Again, I was left with the logic that to go forward might be the end of us, but staying put would definitely be. So I began painfully to put one foot in front of the other.

It took every ounce of strength I had. There was no energy left over for questions or to try to shout loud enough to make myself heard to the person in front of us. They kept walking without looking back at us, and I was terrified that if we fell behind and lost sight of them, we would never find them again.

I have no idea how long we walked. It felt like more than an hour, but none of my senses were working right anymore. The only things I registered were being tired and being cold. The three of us kept stumbling forward behind our mysterious guides like a zombie with three heads. In some places drifts of snow made deep pockets, and Henry would sink into them up to his neck before climbing out. I knew he was getting tired too, and at this point I simply did not have the strength to carry him.

Without warning, Shadow veered away and I instantly lost sight of him in the blowing snow. Panicked, I looked at the person in front of us, who had stopped and was reaching for something. It was only when I saw a yellow rectangle of light that I realized we were standing at the front door of a house.

With what literally might have been the last few steps I had the energy to take, I moved through the doorway, pushing Jack in first, then turning to make sure that Quin was coming in too. Then I stepped in, pulling my exhausted beagle with me. When the door was pulled closed behind us, the sound of the wind was muffled, and I heard ringing in my ears. I noticed only a few details of the house at first. The room was dry, light, and warm. There was a fire burning in a fireplace. And the walls — they were covered in photographs, all of the same thing. Everywhere I looked, I saw them.

The faces of dogs.

No one spoke for a long time. I got my gloves off and fumbled with my zipper, then tried to help Jack with his. My fingers were numb with cold, but I was desperate to get my snow-covered layers off so that I could warm myself by the fire. Henry had instantly collapsed in front of it and was now in a deep sleep, bathed in orange light.

"Jack, your boots," I said. "Are you okay? Here, I'll hold while you pull."

It wasn't until I had both of our boots and fleeces off, and Quin was down to her jeans and sweater, that I realized the person we had followed had pulled off layers of jackets, scarves, and hats as well.

She was a tiny, birdlike woman with iron gray hair and a face creased with age and a lifetime spent out of doors. She nodded toward the fire, placing a kettle to boil on a stove in the corner of the room. The three of us crowded around the fire. Jack held his hands as close as he could to the flames.

"Don't put your hands so close to the fire," Quin warned my brother. "You'll get chilblains."

"What are chillbuns?" Jack mumbled through lips numb with cold.

"When you warm your fingers and toes up too fast after being out in a storm," Quin said. "You get little red blisters, and they really hurt. You don't want 'em."

I watched the old woman taking cups down from a shelf. I didn't know which question to ask her first — where are we? How did you find us? Where is Shadow?

"Thank you," Quin said. Then to emphasize it, she smiled at the woman and nodded.

The woman gave a small nod in return, then opened a tin and began measuring tea leaves into a strainer.

"My fingers hurt already," Jack moaned. "And my toes. Does that mean I have chillbuns now?"

Quin took Jack's hands in hers.

"No. The hurting's actually a good sign," Quin told him. "I know it doesn't feel like it right now, but it is. See how your fingertips are turning bright red? That means they're still healthy. No frostbite. The pain means they're coming back to life."

Jack made a small whimpering sound as she rubbed his fingers briskly between her own, but he didn't snatch his hands away.

"You're going to be okay, kiddo," I said. "We're safe now."

My little brother stared at the old woman, his eyes round.

"Is that the witch?" he asked quietly.

"Jack, don't be rude," I said, though I was wondering the exact same thing. Surely it couldn't be a coincidence that people thought there was a witch living in the woods when here was an old woman, living in the middle of nowhere, miles and miles from another human being.

Luckily, the woman didn't seem to have heard Jack's question. In fact, there was nothing so far to suggest that she could hear at all. She was old, but not that old — she'd just walked us through a blizzard, after all. If I had to guess, I'd put her age around sixty-five or so. She might just be deaf. She did turn back toward the stove when the kettle began to whistle, but maybe she just saw the steam coming out of the spout.

"How did she find us?" I whispered to Quin. "Nobody knew where we were."

Quin shrugged, moving away from the fireplace to scrutinize more of the photos adorning the walls.

What I really wanted to know was why the woman was out in the storm in the first place. Surely grannies didn't just head out for a stroll in the snow, even in Alaska? And what about the dog ghost?

"Tee," Quin said. "Come look at these."

Quin was standing to one side of the fireplace, examining a circle of five oval-shaped photographs hanging on the wall.

"Oh, gosh," I said. "They're gorgeous."

Each photograph was of a different dog. All five of them wore similar harnesses, suggesting they were from the same team. They all looked like huskies or maybe malamutes. Though each was similar in build, something in the way the photographs had been taken brought out the individual in each animal. Just looking at them gave me a feel for their personalities — the darkest one powerful and aloof, the one with the white face affectionate and playful.

"So beautiful," Quin said quietly, reaching out to touch a photo of a snow white dog with mismatched eyes.

I heard the sound of ceramic gently knocking wood, and turned to see the woman pouring mugs of steaming tea. I walked to the small table where she had placed them, taking the first and handing it to Jack. I briefly caught the woman's eye when I picked up the other two.

"Thank you," I said.

Her eyes darted from me to Quin, and back to me again, but she still said nothing.

Though the numbing sensation of cold was now fading, I was still far from warm, and the tea smelled creamy and sweet, and the idea of drinking something hot was irresistible. I carried the mugs to Quin, and handed her one. The two of us sipped at the same time, not caring if we burnt our tongues. I watched the woman while trying to look like I wasn't. She had pulled a thick, heavy blanket out of a wooden trunk near the door. Wordlessly, she carried it to the fireplace and spread it on the floor. Jack, who had been standing there clutching his mug like it was a life preserver, put his tea down and immediately curled up on the blanket.

"Looks like it's still bad out there," I said to Quin, nodding toward the window.

She nodded. "Jack's got the right idea. We might as well get comfortable, 'cause we're not getting out of here anytime soon."

The idea of lying on the blanket by the warmth of the fire was very tempting. But I felt uneasy, almost afraid to let my guard down, as if we'd wandered into some kind of Hansel-and-Gretel scenario. I was probably delusional from being cold and tired, but I could not get the idea out of my head that this woman was indeed the witch. On a simple chest of drawers in the corner sat a single photograph. The others on the wall were all clustered together in plain wooden frames, but this one was in a lovely silver frame. Another detail set this picture apart — it was the only photograph in the room with a person in it: a little girl, her arms wrapped around the neck of a dog. I walked over to get a better look. Was I dreaming, or hallucinating from the cold? I closed my eyes, then opened them again.

"It's him," I whispered, picking up the photograph. "Quin, look, it's Shadow!"

Before Quin could respond, the woman crossed the room with remarkable speed. She snatched the picture from my hands, and I stepped back quickly. Her blue eyes blazed.

"I'm sorry," I stammered. "I didn't mean . . . I was only —"

"Did you see him?" she asked.

My mouth moved but I couldn't make any sound come out. The intensity of the woman's look, the fire in her eyes, and the unexpected arrival of her voice addled me. I felt as if the room were spinning, as if I might fall.

The old woman grabbed my arm, not to steady me but to get an answer out of me.

"For the love of Pete, move your lips. Tell me what you saw."

Her grip on my arm loosened, and her eyes grew shiny with tears.

"Tell me what you saw, child," she repeated more quietly. "Did you see my dog? Did you see my Caspian?"

13

"I . . . Caspian?" I asked.

The woman nodded. I tried to catch Quin's eye, but I couldn't see around the woman, whose fierce gaze frightened me, though I somehow knew she meant me no harm. Everything about this was strange — dreamlike — a woman living alone out here in a cottage filled with pictures of dogs. My fear suddenly left me. In my core, I felt that we were meant to be here — that the mystery of the dog ghost was on the brink of being solved.

"Yes," I told her. "I saw him. We thought he was . . . His name is Caspian?"

She nodded, her eyes half-closed.

"And was he . . . well, was he your dog, ma'am?" I pressed gently.

She nodded. "Yes, he was mine. We had a great many dogs, but that one was special. Caspian was my heart dog."

Quin had moved into view from behind the woman. Her eyes met mine.

"And my name is Dodie, not ma'am," she added.

"I'm Tee, and this is my friend Quin," I told her. "And that's my little brother, Jack."

Jack was curled up like a puppy on the blanket by the fire, both hands resting under his cheek, fast asleep, Henry snoring beside him.

"And the beagle?" she asked.

"He's mine," I said. "His name is Henry."

I knew I didn't need to ask this woman if it was okay that I'd brought a dog inside. She was looking at Henry, with eyes that suddenly sparked with interest.

"Henry," she repeated. "Good name for a beagle. We'll rustle him up some grub when he wakes up."

"Thank you," I told Dodie. "For everything, I mean. You might have saved our lives. How did you know we were out there — how did you find us?"

"Wasn't me that found you," Dodie said. "Caspian did that."

Her eyes filled with tears again, and she pressed her lips together, returned the picture to its spot on the chest of drawers, and walked toward the stove.

I thought this was her way of telling us the subject of Caspian was closed, but she pulled a second chair up to the kitchen table and dragged over a small wooden crate to act as a third. When she placed the kettle back on the stove, I knew she wanted us to come and sit at the table with her. Something had shifted in her manner, in her energy. She was talking now, and she was going to keep talking.

She told us the story of Caspian.

Quin and I listened, enraptured, as Dodie recalled a painful story of a misunderstood dog that she and her sister loved more than any dog in the world. Of how her sister went missing in a storm, and the dog, Caspian, was blamed for it.

"That's most of it, I suppose," Dodie said, her eyes unfocused and far away. "Oh, I'm not some crazy old hermit. I get into town every now and again. Clyde's son brings me up groceries and supplies. This is where I am, and this is where I'll stay until I die, and I can see Silla and Caspian again. And about a week ago, I thought I was doing just that — dying, I mean. Because I opened my front door and there was Caspian, plain as day, off near the old trail to the creek."

Quin and I exchanged a look. There were so many puzzle pieces here, and I thought I was on the verge of

165

understanding, but I wasn't there yet. And neither, from her expression, was Quin.

"Did Caspian see you too?" Quin asked.

"Oh, yes," Dodie said, nodding. "He was looking right at me, then he turned and trotted off. I grabbed my coat and followed him, but I couldn't pick up his trail, and just like that he was gone. The next day, he showed up again. Every day for a week, Caspian has been waiting when I open my door. And this time he let me keep up with him, and I did, even as the wind picked up and the snow started coming down like crazy. I followed him all the way to that old cabin, right to the doorway. And that's where your part of the story comes in."

Dodie looked at me and I sat up very straight in my chair, suddenly understanding.

"Caspian led you to us," I said. "You saved us because Caspian knew where we were and took you there."

"That's right," Dodie said, her eyes shining. "And here you are, and you come telling me that you've seen Caspian too."

I nodded. Suddenly, I understood.

"We have," I said. "But we were calling him Shadow."

"Shadow?" Dodie asked. "Well, that fits, I suppose. He looked like one, and that's what he's been, more or less, all these years. But how did you see him? Where? Please try to tell me everything that you know about him."

I told her about my first outing with Henry.

"And then Quin came with me, and we found the old cabin. Caspian was there." Dodie looked at Quin curiously.

"That's where you found him? How odd. Silla and I used to play in that cabin when we were girls. It's going to collapse, though — one good storm could bring it down. It's not a safe place for anyone to be. What was Caspian doing there?" she asked.

"I felt like maybe he was guarding something," Quin said.

I nodded. "I thought that too. And later, neither of us could get him out of our heads. We felt like he needed help. And then one night at dinner Clay brought all these old pictures of dogs over to Quin's house."

"Not Clay Nolan?" Dodie asked.

"That's right," Quin said. "Do you know him?"

Dodie gave a short laugh. "Everybody who lives in Nome and has ever worked with dogs knows Clay. His brother, Vernon, worked for my father handling the dogs. He used to live right here in this cottage, actually. Clay's good people."

"He is," Quin said warmly. "Well, Clay brought over folders of old photos of sled dogs. Tee and I took them upstairs and started going through them — it seems crazy now but we thought we might find our ghost dog there."

"It's not really crazy," Dodie told her. "Clay's probably photographed half the dogs that ever ran the Iditarod, and plenty more that didn't. My folks always had someone take pictures of their dogs — that's what all these are. You had good instincts."

"And now we know there *was* a picture of Caspian," I said, pointing to the picture on the chest of drawers. "But we didn't find anything. Except . . ." I laughed, shaking my head. "At one point we found a picture of Balto and we thought we'd found our dog ghost. It's so stupid, but that's what we thought."

"It's not stupid at all," Dodie said. "Balto was one of Seppala's dogs, and I told you our Siberians came from the same line as his. Balto and Caspian were related. Not father and son or anything like that, but distantly. You're not the first to think Caspian bore a resemblance to Balto."

"Wow," I said. "That's kind of incredible."

"But back to your story," Dodie said.

"Well, we decided if we couldn't find a picture of the dog ghost, maybe we could go back to the cabin and take a picture of him. And that might help us figure out where he'd come from. And when he'd come from."

168

"That's how we ended up at the old cabin," Quin said. "We had started home because Caspian wasn't there. When we got caught in the snow we doubled back to hole up in the cabin till the weather passed."

"Smart young lady," Dodie said. "With the whiteout, you'd never have been able to separate snow from sky. You'd have gotten lost, wandering out there. Frozen to death."

I gulped.

"And that's when you found us," I said. "We'd been there awhile, probably a couple of hours. The cabin didn't give much shelter. We were so cold and so tired, and in the end I just wanted to go to sleep."

"It's a good thing you didn't," Dodie said. "I expect that's how it went with Silla — she just gave in and let sleep take her." Dodie let out a long breath and stared at the fireplace. "All these years gone, then Caspian comes back. He gets me and brings me to you."

"He couldn't save Silla, but he saved us," Quin said.

Dodie pressed her hand to her mouth.

"Oh, Caspian," she said quietly.

The three of us sat in silence, the only sound the pop and hiss of the crackling fire. Jack was still curled up in a ball, lost in a deep sleep.

"Then you've solved my puzzle, I suppose," Dodie told

me. "Caspian came back because he had to — because there were children that needed saving."

"I think there's more to it than that," Quin said suddenly.

"More how?" Dodie asked.

"You said Caspian had been coming to your door every day for the last week," Quin said, and Dodie nodded.

"Well, we didn't need saving then. And it was less than a week ago that Henry got spooked by Caspian, which in turn led Tee and me to the cabin. You said you stopped catching glimpses of Caspian after that first year, and that he went away. And that he's come back now. But what if he hasn't come back, Dodie? What if he's been here all along?"

"But why?" Dodie asked.

Something in what Quin said made sense to me. I understood what she was getting at. I chimed in.

"Other than you, Dodie, and now us, has anyone that you're aware of ever seen Caspian all these years? Has anyone thought there was a wild dog living in the woods?"

Dodie shook her head

"Because not everyone can," I continued. "Quin said there are stories about people glimpsing a shadow in the woods up here. But that's all it is — a glimpse — not enough for anyone to even know what they're seeing. Quin is really good with dogs. I guess we both are. Maybe that's it. But whatever it was — we saw Caspian because we *could* see him. And somehow he knew that — he realized we were different. I think Quin and I sort of woke him up a bit. After all these years someone was speaking to him. So he went to get you. Quin's right — Caspian didn't leave and come back. He's been out there all along. Whatever he was trying to do fifty or however many years ago when your father ran him off, he's still trying to do it."

Dodie had fixed me with a gaze so intense I almost drew back.

"Trying to do what?"

I hesitated, looking to Quin. She gave a small nod, and I knew she was thinking the same thing I was.

"I think maybe Caspian knows where Silla is," I said quietly.

I don't know what reaction I was expecting — maybe anger or shock, but Dodie never took her eyes off mine. She rubbed her mouth again, once, then she placed her hand palm down on the table.

"Of course Caspian would know where Silla is," Dodie said. "I've never had any doubt that he was with her until the very end."

"But you were the only one who believed that," Quin said. "As far as everyone else knew, Caspian was a murderer. People were as good as out there hunting him, you said so yourself. You were the only one who believed in Caspian after Silla went missing. And he knew that. So he stayed."

"Stayed and hid?" Dodie asked. "If he thought I needed protecting, which he would have known I didn't, why didn't he just make himself plain?"

"I don't think you were the one he was protecting," Quin said.

"Caspian was protecting Silla," Dodie whispered. "For a half century. No one ever found her, and he's still keeping watch."

"Yes," Quin said quietly. "And he's going to keep guarding her until Silla is found, and he knows she's safe. She's home. Somewhere near that cabin."

"The cabin?" Dodie asked. "No, that isn't right. Silla told me that morning she was going to look for gold in the pool. That part of the creek is at least five miles from the cabin. She was nowhere near it."

"But is it possible Silla changed her mind?" I asked. Dodie looked at me sharply. "I mean, maybe she headed out for the pool, but changed her mind and went toward the cabin instead?"

Dodie narrowed her eyes in thought, her eyebrows creased. "I don't . . . I never thought . . . oh, heavens. I don't think so. But why not? She could have done, she might have changed her mind. Maybe she decided to save the gold hunt for a warmer day. But how can I ever know that now?"

The mention of gold jarred something in my memory. I found my coat where Dodie had hung it near the fire, and fished in the pocket.

"Jack found this in the cabin," I said, handing her the little golden button.

Dodie took it from me and held it up to the firelight, her expression unreadable. Then I saw all the color leave her face.

"This was Silla's," she whispered.

Dodie stood up and crossed the room, taking Caspian's picture in her hands.

"Why did I never think she might have gone to the cabin?" She turned to look at the two of us. "It was where we went to play when we wanted to share a secret, or we wanted to be well and truly left alone. Hidden. The roof was sagging even then, but we found a little trapdoor in the floor — a wooden hatch, and underneath it was a hole someone had dug, just a simple root cellar, really, to keep ice and things. We used to put treasures down there."

173

"Treasures?" Quin asked.

"That's what we called them. Just little bits of things we had in our pockets or from the kennel. A bit of ribbon, or a marble, that sort of thing. A golden button," she added, staring at the one in her hand.

"So she took off with Caspian, but decided to go to the cabin instead of the pool," I said. "And when the storm came she climbed into the root cellar for shelter?"

Dodie nodded. "I think so. It's what I would have done — it was the smart thing to do. But she couldn't have known the storm would last three days. Even down in that little cellar out of the wind, she would still have been overtaken by the cold and the damp. Her lungs couldn't handle that. Not even with Caspian down there helping to keep her warm."

"So he stayed with her until she . . . until she went to sleep. Could he have gotten out by himself after?"

"Certainly. Caspian was an extremely intelligent dog. Most of Seppala's Siberians were. Once he knew Silla was gone, he could easily have nudged the door open with his nose and leapt out. I suppose the door slammed shut behind him. With all the people searching the woods, someone must have gone by the cabin and looked inside — but no one would have thought to poke around for that old door. We didn't think she was there."

"And that day when you and your father saw Caspian?" I asked.

"He had probably just left her," Dodie said. "And hadn't eaten in three days — he probably pounced on the first rabbit he saw."

"And your father jumped to conclusions when he saw the blood, and never stopped to realize Caspian was trying to lead you to the cabin," I said.

"Yes," Dodie said, very quietly.

"I'm so sorry," Quin said.

Dodie replaced the picture on the chest, and turned to me. She smiled, the first real smile we'd seen.

"On the contrary," Dodie said. "You can't imagine what this means to me. To know what happened, after all these years. To finally understand. I feel happier than I have in years. And I know what I need to do now."

"I'm glad Caspian found us," Quin said.

"So am I," Dodie said. "Especially today of all days. Living in Nome, Quin, you ought to know better than to wander off when bad weather is on the way. Surely you were raised with more sense than that."

Quin gasped with dismay.

"Tee, they don't know where we are!" Quin cried.

I jumped to my feet.

"We have to go," I said. "We have to go right now."

"The snow hasn't stopped, you can't go yet," Dodie said.

"You don't understand — my father will be sick with worry. If he got home and found us gone, he'd . . ."

My voice trailed off as I realized Dodie knew exactly how my father would feel.

"It's all right," Dodie said. "I'm only sorry I kept you talking for an hour before thinking of it. I did tell you I'm not a crazy old hermit lady."

She pulled open the top drawer of the chest as she spoke, and pulled something out.

"I think this will do the trick," she said.

"What is it?" I asked.

Dodie smiled. "Really, child, use your eyes. It's a satellite phone."

14

I was sure my father would be ready to string me up by the time we reached him on Dodie's satellite phone. He and Joe had taken Joe's snowmobile and headed for our cabin. They had been stunned and completely powerless to do anything when they'd reached it and found all three of us missing. But by the time I got the call through, he was so overcome with relief that he didn't yell at all.

"You're sure all three of you are all right?" he kept asking, over and over again.

"Dad, we're fine," I repeated. "I'm just so, so sorry — all of this is my fault."

"We both know that's not entirely true," he said. "Anyway, all that matters is you're all okay. Listen, it's still blowing badly, and we can't get you out of there today. Joe's made a plan. He and Clay and I will each take a snowmobile out to you tomorrow — that way we can get all three of you back here at the same time. You're just going to have to hold Henry on your lap, unless he can run alongside."

"Cool," I said, thinking it was going to be pretty funny to see Dad driving a snowmobile, and wondering how I could make sure I was the passenger on Clay's.

When I hung up I explained the plan to Quin and Dodie.

"You two had best get some rest, then," Dodie said. "Your brother is still fast asleep. I've got more blankets and some pillows."

"How long were they looking for us?" Quin asked.

"Dad said they got up to the cabin about an hour earlier. Probably about the same time we got to Dodie's. So they'd been freaking out for that whole hour."

"Well, it could have been a lot worse," Quin said. "If Dodie didn't have a satellite phone, we'd be unaccounted for until we were able to get back tomorrow. I hope your dad's not too mad at you."

"Actually, he wasn't that mad at all," I told her. "He practically apologized to me, said it was his fault."

"Really?" she asked.

I nodded.

"Well, hey. Looks like more than one unexpected thing happened today."

"You'll have to make do with these," Dodie said.

She'd piled a fat goose-down comforter and a quilt by the fire, pulling them carefully over Jack. A few small pillows had been laid out.

"The two of you must be exhausted," Dodie remarked, fussing a little with the corner of the quilt.

As soon as she said it, I realized how right she was. I was more tired than I'd ever been in my life.

Quin and I climbed into the makeshift bed carefully, with me in the middle next to Jack. As soon as Quin's head hit the pillow, I swear I heard snoring. I drew the comforter up to my chin and took a deep breath. I wanted to let my mind run over everything that had happened today, everything Dodie had told us. But I knew I'd be asleep before I could do that.

Jack rolled over so he was facing me, and his eyes opened sleepily.

"Tee?" he asked. "Whassgoinon?"

"Nothing, Jackster," I said quietly. "Go back to sleep."

"Long as I don't miss anything," he murmured, the last syllable falling off into nothing.

I smiled, snuggled deeper under the blankets, and followed my little brother to sleep.

179

The three of us were sitting around Dodie's kitchen table eating oatmeal for breakfast when we first heard the sound of approaching snowmobiles. Jack raced to the window.

"Whoa, there's *three* of them," he exclaimed. "No! Way! Tee, one of the drivers is Dad!"

I joined Jack at the window and watched with amusement. Joe and Clay had gotten off their snowmobiles, but my dad apparently needed some help figuring out how to turn his off. I'd be amazed if he hadn't taken out a couple of trees along the way.

"I'll get some water going so they can have tea," Dodie said.

"I'm sorry you're having to deal with all these people," I apologized. If Dodie had been living here alone for more or less fifty years, having six people in her home must be overwhelming.

"I'll manage," Dodie said. I had no trouble believing that.

There was knocking at the door, which Jack pulled open triumphantly, as if he were responsible for all of it — the storm, the rescue, and the snowmobiles, everything. Joe came in next, and instantly crushed Quin in a bear hug. My father put one arm around my shoulders, the other around Jack.

"Thank goodness you're all okay," he said.

"It was my fault, though," I told him, my face pressed into his sleeve.

"We can talk about how it happened later, if you want. The point is, you're okay. It's a miracle you found this place —"

His voice dropped off as he looked around the cottage and took in all the pictures of the sled dogs.

"Tee," he said quietly, "what *is* this place?"

"It's Dodie's cottage, Dad. She lives out here. She saved us."

My father crossed to the corner, entranced by the photographs.

"Dorothy Shaktoolik?" Clay's voice came from the doorway.

Dodie turned from the stove.

"Clayton Nolan," she said. "Are you gonna shut that door, or are we gonna have icicles in our tea?"

Clay pulled the door closed, and pulled off his hat and boots.

"Well hey, Doe. I heard something about you still living out here in Vernon's old place," he said. "But frankly, I thought those stories was crazy."

"Who's to say they're not?" Dodie said, smiling at Clay, with sparkling eyes. He smiled back.

Quin and I exchanged a look and tiny smiles that said, *What's going on there?*

"I'm afraid there's far more of you than there are chairs," Dodie said.

"You guys sit at the table, we'll sit on the floor," I said quickly.

"But I don't wanna —" I silenced Jack by squeezing the back of his neck a little.

"Ow."

Quin, Jack, and I sat by the fire on the blankets and comforter we had folded when we got up.

"If that's hot tea you've got there, I'd sure love a cup," Joe said. "And I'm quite frankly dying to hear what exactly happened to these kids yesterday."

We took turns telling the story, describing the cabin, the sudden arrival of snow, taking shelter. How we thought we'd freeze, and the snow was blowing in and covering us, when Dodie found us and led us back to her cottage. The only detail we left out was the most important one. We did not say anything about Caspian. That was Dodie's story, one she might well not care to have shared with others. Even Jack seemed to realize this, because most of his contributions to the story involved fingers and toes that almost fell off, and his own brave behavior in the face of certain death.

"And I brought them back here, and fixed them up with some hot tea and blankets, and was glad for the company, if you want the truth," Dodie was saying.

Joe had one hand over his eyes.

"Quin, sweetie, that was a close call for you guys. If you'd had to spend the night in that cabin . . ."

"I know," Quin said, getting up off the floor and walking over to the table where her father sat. "I knew I was supposed to check the weather, and I . . . we were in a hurry and I just flat out forgot. I'm really, really sorry."

"But she did the right thing holing up in the cabin," Dodie said. "She bought them a lot of time — enough for me to happen by and find them. And I guess they're no worse for the wear, and I've had enough excitement to last me a year."

"You've been out here all this time in Vernon's old place?" asked Clay.

Dodie nodded.

"I come into town once or twice a year, when Clyde can run up and get me," she said. "And Pete Jr. brings me mail and supplies. We have a bit of a get-together every now and again. But I was raised here, Clay, you know that. And I like the quiet."

"I guess it's a good enough little house," Clay said, looking around the room. Something caught his eye, and he rose and walked over to the chest of drawers.

"My stars, Doe, is this Caspian? And Silla?"

I stared at Clay in astonishment. How did he know Caspian? And I had assumed the girl in the picture was Dodie.

"Yes, it is."

Clay shook his head sadly.

"That was a terrible thing," he said. "Seeing Caspian's face it all comes back. Your father was just out of his mind with sadness when Silla went missing. But you know, I never believed that dog hurt anyone, let alone Silla. Didn't believe it then, and don't believe it now."

Dodie sat rigid in her chair, her eyes on Clay, a tear rolling down her cheek.

"Oh, Clay, I wish you'd said so. All these years I thought I was the only one who believed in Caspian."

Clay came back to the table, put a hand on Dodie's shoulder.

"I'm sure it wasn't just me," he assured her. "Martin and Ike and all those fellows agreed when your daddy told them

Caspian was dangerous and ought to be shot. But I don't think none of them really believed it. I expect they knew your father was too hurt in his heart and was taking it out on the dog. Not one of them ever went out in the woods with their shotguns looking for Caspian, not that they told me, anyway. I figure that's just something they told your daddy to ease his pain a little."

Dodie put her hand to her face for a moment, then looked up at Clay.

"All these years I thought everyone blamed him," she said.

"I don't expect that's true," Clay said, sitting back down.

Quin and I were now staring at Clay and Dodie with our mouths hanging open.

"Clay, how did you know Caspian?" Quin blurted out, and I almost hugged her because I could stand the anticipation no longer.

Clay turned around and looked at Quin as if he'd completely forgotten she was there — or that anyone was, except for Dodie.

"My brother, Vernon, used to be one of the dog handlers when the Shaktooliks had their kennel out here," he said. "I came out every once in a while to give Vernon a hand with things, have a look at the dogs. At least, that's what I told everybody. Truth is I was kind of sweet on Doe here, but I was a whole year younger than her, just sixteen years old and tall and skinny and ugly as a grasshopper and she wouldn't have nothing to do with me."

Dodie flushed red, accentuating the lovely blue of her eyes.

"He's just poking fun," she said.

"No, I ain't," Clay said firmly.

Dodie dismissed him with a wave of her hand, and got up to put the kettle back on. But I got a glimpse of her expression as she turned, and to say she looked happy was quite an understatement.

"Much as we'd love to have another cup, I think we better get these kids back home," Joe said.

"I guess Joe's right," my father said. "But Ms. Shaktoolik . . ."

"Dodie," she corrected. Then she pointed at Clay. "Only he calls me Doe."

"Dodie," my father said. "You've obviously got an incredible history of raising dogs. I already owe you the lives of my children, so I have no business asking you for anything else, but if there's any chance you'd let me come back up here and interview you, maybe find out more about these dogs, I'd be so incredibly grateful to you. I don't have a snowmobile, but if I could rent one I'd be happy to come and bring you anything you need at the same time."

"No need for that, I can bring you up myself," Clay said.

Dodie seemed to go red again.

"Well, I guess that might be all right," she said.

Clay smiled at her, his whole face illuminated like it was shining from within.

"Oh, that's great, really great," my father said. "This is exactly the chance I've been looking for — this is why we came to Alaska in the first place."

"Kids, you'd better start getting bundled up," Joe said. "It is really cold out there."

We reluctantly left the fire and began layering on the fleeces and hats that we'd taken off the night before. Quin and I had to get our own on first, then maneuver Jack into his, since he seemed to have forgotten how to operate sleeves and zippers. After several long minutes we were more or less ready and standing by the door. I ran to Dodie and gave her a long hug, and she hugged me right back, and her grip was pretty tight. It didn't surprise me that she was way stronger than she looked.

"Thank you," I murmured. "Can we come back to see you?"

Dodie smiled.

"I guess you better," she said.

We had all walked outside into the brilliant sunlight and

the bitter cold, when Clay stopped and turned around. Dodie was standing in the open doorway.

"You know somethin', Doe, Whit Haverson's got two litters of pups right now — one of 'em was a winter litter. They're about, oh, almost three months now. He's been telling me how one's a bit of a runt, and is getting awful bullied by the others now as they're getting bigger. He's not gonna be able to train this little guy with the team, and he says truth is that dog could be a great dog if he wasn't getting pushed around so much. It's hard on his spirit being trounced by the rest of the litter all the time. A dog like that, I figure, could probably do with a spell away from other dogs, if there was only someplace for him to go."

Dodie stood staring at Clay, who stood staring back.

"What's his name?" Dodie asked.

"Haverson just calls him Sam," Clay said. "Gray and white, with a little black smudge under one eye, his own personal shiner. Says he's small but smart as a whip. He's just a little frustrated from getting whupped by his brothers and sisters every time he turns around."

Dodie put a hand on her mouth, then reached up and smoothed the hair away from her face.

"You tell Whit he can send that pup out here, if he'd like," Dodie said. "I can sort him out."

"I think he'll be awful relieved to have someone help him out with the little guy," Clay told her. He glanced at me and Quin, and winked.

"That's settled, then, and you'd best get a move on before you get caught in another blizzard," Dodie said. "And you've drunk all my tea, so you're on your own."

"I'll bring some," Clay said. "Next time."

"And who invited you back, Clayton Nolan?" Dodie called.

"Well, nobody, but I figure Sam and Tee's dad here are gonna need a ride," Clay said. "I guess I could throw in a couple slices of cake to sweeten the deal."

Dodie made a little waving gesture and closed the door, more shooing us away than saying good-bye.

We were all smiling as we climbed onto the snowmobiles, and although the air was bitterly cold and we all covered our faces with scarves, I, for one, kept smiling beneath the layers all the way home.

15

I banged on the door.

"Quin! QUIN!" I yelled.

I wanted to stomp my foot with frustration. Where was she?

"Just one more minute," I called to my dad, who was sitting in the car waiting for me. "She's got to be home — where else would she be?"

I knocked again.

"Quin!"

"Geez, why don't you yell loud enough to wake the dead?" called a voice from down the street.

I turned to see Quin leaning out the front door two houses down — Clay's house.

"Hey!" I called back.

"Come on over here to Clay's," Quin shouted. "Guess who's here — Sam! He's sooo cute — come meet him!"

I ran to the car. "Dad, can I go over to Clay's with Quin and meet Sam the puppy?"

"Oh, isn't Clay taking him up to Dodie's today? Sure, go on. I can pick you up later on my way back."

"I want to see the puppy too!" yelled Jack from the backseat.

My father turned around to look at him.

"Yeah?" he asked. "More than you want to see the 3-D dinosaur shark movie?"

Jack looked genuinely flummoxed.

"Well, nope," he said. "But in a different way. I want to see them both!"

"So you and I will go the movie like we planned," my father told him. "And when Sam's settled in with Dodie, we'll borrow a couple of snowmobiles and go up there to visit."

"Can I drive a snowmobile?" Jack cried. "Can I?"

I grinned.

"Good luck handling that one," I said. "See you later."

"See you later," Dad repeated. "Oh, and Tee? Have fun."

"I will," I told him. "Thanks."

He gave me a little nod. In the best of times my father was not that big of a talker. He communicated best through the written word. But a lot had been communicated between the two of us since the blizzard two days earlier. Already, I could see the difference it was going to make in our lives.

I ran the short distance down the street, to where Quin was still standing impatiently in the doorway.

"Come on," she called. "Sam is so cute. You're gonna die!"

She held the door open and I dashed inside, excited to see the famous Sam, and full of my own good news.

"Hey there, Tee," Clay called. "Come meet this young fella."

Clay was sitting on the floor with a small, sleek husky who was watching him attentively. The dog was dark gray on top, but his chest, stomach, and legs were white. Both of his ears were jet-black, and when he turned his head to look at me, I could see the spot of black under one eye that Clay had described.

"Sam, stay," Clay said.

Sam instantly turned his attention back to Clay, appearing to be concentrating with every cell in his little body. His tail wagged hopefully.

"Good boy, Sam," Clay said, tossing the puppy a treat.

Sam jumped up, caught and swallowed the treat, then immediately sat back down again to stare hard at Clay.

"Oh, Haverson was right, this pup's as smart as they come," Clay said. "Come on over, Tee, meet him up close in person. He won't bite. Actually, maybe he will, but only puppy nibbles!"

I walked over and knelt next to Sam, who smelled deliciously of the special scent of puppies — kibble and newspaper and puppy breath.

"Hi there, buddy," I said, scratching his ears. "Boy, do I know a bored beagle I left in the cabin who'd like to meet you!"

"That would be good for him," Quin said. "You should bring Henry out to Dodie's once Sam gets settled in. Except it will probably be time for you to go home by then," she added, her eyes darkening.

"You're going back to New York?" Clay asked. "That's a shame."

"Well, our plan was only to stay two weeks," I said. "It overlapped with spring break at our school, even though we still missed a week. And my dad spent two whole days with Dodie and it apparently completely got him going on his book. She's letting him use photographs, the old logbooks and diaries from the kennel, everything he wants. And guess what?" I said, turning to face Quin, my eyes shining.

"You're moving here?" Quin asked hopefully.

"Well, sorry, no," I said. "But it's something you'll like. Dodie told Dad the whole story about Caspian. He was totally enthralled with it. He thought it was a perfect example of how dogs and humans can bond, but also how people still don't fully understand dog behavior — even people who have worked with them all their lives can make a mistake. So get this — he asked Dodie if he could tell Caspian's story — and not just tell it — he wants to start the whole book with the story. Plus, he wants to use the photo of Caspian and Silla as the cover. And Dodie said okay!"

"That's amazing!" Quin exclaimed. "Now everybody will know Caspian's story — his real story!"

"Oh yes," Clay said, a little gruffly. "That's . . . well, that's a gift I didn't think anybody could give Dodie. That'll just mean the whole world to her. Give her some peace."

"Can we tell Tee about the other thing?" Quin asked.

Clay nodded, nudging Sam so that he rolled over to have his tummy scratched.

"Clay and some of Dodie's family, Clyde and Pete Jr., went with Dodie yesterday to the cabin and cleared away all the rubble. They got the trapdoor open, and Silla's bones are down there, just like Dodie thought. They need to meet with somebody from the government to get permission, but they're going to be able to bury Silla in a real grave, on Dodie's land."

"Oh," I breathed. "That's what Caspian wanted — that's what he's been waiting for — for Silla to be found!"

"That's just so," Clay agreed. "And I didn't tell you the last part yet, Quin. Doe called me up on her space-phone thing this morning."

"She did?" Quin said, making google eyes at me when she thought Clay couldn't see.

"Yes, she did," Clay said. "Asked me if I'd give her a hand training Sam, here. Maybe think about rounding up a few other pups folks has that aren't fitting in. Who knows, maybe we'll get a team together."

"That would be amazing," Quin exclaimed, her eyes shining. "If you do, would you teach me to run them?"

"We'd need you to," Clay said. "Doe and I are a bit old to be doing too much of that. But you get a team in shape, Quin, you could enter 'em in the Junior Iditarod."

"There's a Junior Iditarod?" I asked.

Quin nodded, grinning wildly. "There is — a big race just for kids and their teams!"

"You are so lucky," I said. "Maybe I can come back for it!"

"That would be so cool," Quin said. "It's going to be so lonely around here with you gone — especially if Clay is spending all this time out at Dodie's."

Clay's face suddenly went red, and he bent over Sam and rubbed the exposed underside of his muzzle.

"There's actually one more thing I have to tell you," I said, unable to stop the huge smile crossing my face. "A happy thing."

"What?" Quin asked. "You said you weren't moving here."

"I'm not," I replied. "But my dad wants to spend more time with Dodie — he's talking about unearthing the ruins of the old kennel, having a photographer come up and document it. Basically, he's decided to keep renting the cabin, and to come back up here for the summer. He said Jack and I could each decide if we wanted to stay in New York or come back here with him."

"Tee, speak in shorter sentences. Are you going to be here this summer?"

"I am!" I exclaimed.

Quin made a high-pitched squeal of delight and hugged me, and I squealed too. Then a high, piercing sound made us let go of each other and look around.

Sam had gotten to his feet and was standing next to us, his little head thrown back, a high puppy howl singing from his throat.

"What's he saying?" I asked, laughing.

"Same thing as you and Quin, I guess," Clay said.

"He's saying he's happy," Quin said. "He feels like good things are happening. He feels like his life is going to be a little different now, and he likes it."

I stroked Sam's sleek, smooth head, and looked into his brown eyes. He looked back at me, and I felt like he could see into me a little. Like he could tap into something that couldn't be expressed very well in words, but that I was saying loudly anyway.

That I would be coming back again, would have the whole summer with Quin, and Clay, and Dodie. That in some way, I had helped Caspian to let go, and that Dodie's world had opened up because of it. That good things were happening.

And I was happy.

DODIE

I don't know when I'd seen so many people at the same time, all of them right there in my cottage. And old Clayton Nolan, of all people. He's as handsome now as he was when he was a boy. I only hope he didn't notice how my heart almost jumped right out of my chest when he walked through that door.

It was so quiet after they all left and the buzzing of the snowmobiles had died away. I was just about knackered from all the goings-on, but I waited until dark to start getting ready for bed, just like always. It was then that I heard the bark. So I went to the door and opened it up. I knew he was there before I saw him.

Caspian was sitting just ten feet or so from the door, and the moon was so bright and full I could see him plain as day. He didn't do anything, he just sat there in the snow looking at me. I looked right back at him, until the picture of his face was so clear in my mind I knew I'd never forget it. And then he just got up, and he walked toward the place where the trees began in long lines of moonshadows. It was only then I realized Caspian had not come alone.

Silla was standing near the trees, the same little wisp of a girl I remembered, her hair silvery in the moonlight. Her face shone like the moon itself — everything about her seemed illuminated from the inside as well as the outside. She raised one hand and waved at me, reaching her other hand toward Caspian, who was now sitting at her feet.

I could not speak, but I didn't have to. I raised my hand too, and waved at my sister. A smile lit her face, and the pureness of her beauty almost broke my heart with happiness. Caspian stood up, and began walking toward the woods. Silla paused a moment, her hand still raised, the ethereal smile still on her lips. Then she followed our dog, and they disappeared together, side by side, swallowed up by the shadows.

I was alone again. But I would not be for long.

Tomorrow I would begin getting the cottage ready for Sam, the puppy. Caspian will always be my heart dog — he took up all the space there I had to love a dog, and I never wanted for company all the years I lived alone.

Not while he was still nearby. I know I won't see Caspian again, not in this lifetime. But I have peace with that. Caspian brought me the children, and he brought me Clay, and he brought my Silla back to me.

Whatever else had happened to him while he was alive, Caspian knew that there were two girls who loved him best, and who always believed in the goodness of his heart.

Now after so many years, I saw how Caspian had thanked us. And now that I understood him, he had gone home at last. No dog ever deserved a better rest.

Lucky Dog
Twelve Tales of Rescued Dogs

Featuring stories from a pack of your favorite authors!

Lucky Dog features sweet and silly stories about playful pups and the kids who love them by some of your favorite authors!

Randi Barrow • Marlane Kennedy
Elizabeth Cody Kimmel • Kirby Larson
C. Alexander London • Leslie Margolis
Jane B. Mason & Sarah Hines Stephens • Ellen Miles
Michael Northrop • Teddy Slater
Tui T. Sutherland • Allan Woodrow

A MYSTERIOUS DOG BRINGS A THRILLING ADVENTURE.

Secret of the Mountain Dog

ELIZABETH CODY KIMMEL

Just when Jax needs a little excitement, a beautiful, giant dog shows up at her door and leads her to an old monastery at the top of the mountain. There she meets a boy who has come all the way from Tibet to search for a long-lost statue. But someone else is searching for the statue, too, and the new friends soon find themselves in danger.

scholastic.com

Scholastic Press
SCRTDOG